"Make a sound and we're both dead."

A scream caught in her throat as she was grabbed from behind. A hand clamped over her mouth as a strong arm circled her waist tightly and she was dragged back through the dark velvet drapery to slam against the rock-hard body of the man.

A man Rory had now known *intimately*. Being this close to the groomsman again, she suddenly felt things she didn't want to feel – especially when she was terrified they'd be caught red-handed breaking and entering, in a compromising position no less!

His breath tickled her ear. His body, so close she could feel way too much of him. She shivered and he drew her even tighter against him as if to keep her warm. The gesture touched her. Until she reminded herself that the man was holding her captive behind the drapes in the royal quarters – and, like her, he apparently had no business here.

Available in May 2010
from Mills & Boon® Intrigue

MONTANA ROYALTY

BY
BJ DANIELS

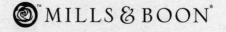

All the characters in this book have no existence outside the imagination of
the author, and have no relation whatsoever to anyone bearing the same name
or names. They are not even distantly inspired by any individual known or
unknown to the author, and all the incidents are pure invention.

First published in Great Britain 2010
Harlequin Mills & Boon Limited,
Eton House, 18-24 Paradise Road, Richm

© Barbara Heinlein 2008

ISBN: 978 0 263 88225 4

46-0510

Harlequin Mills & Boon policy is to use p
and recyclable products and made from wood grown in sustainable forests.
The logging and manufacturing processes conform to the legal environmental
regulations of the country of origin.

Printed and bound in Spain
by Litografia Rosés S.A., Barcelona

ROM
Pbk

BJ Daniels wrote her first book after a career as an award-winning newspaper journalist and author of thirty-seven published short stories. Since then she has won numerous awards, including a career achievement award for romantic suspense, and received many nominations and awards for best book.

BJ lives in Montana with her husband, Parker, and two springer spaniels, Spot and Jem. When she isn't writing, she snowboards, camps, boats and plays tennis. She is a member of Mystery Writers of America, Sisters in Crime, Thriller Writers, Kiss of Death and Romance Writers of America.

To contact her, write to BJ Daniels, PO Box 1173, Malta, MT 59538, USA or e-mail her at bjdaniels@mtintouch. net. Check out her web page at www.bjdaniels.com.

Chapter One

The narrow slit of light between the partially closed bedroom curtains drew him through the shadowed pines.

He moved stealthily, the moonless darkness heavy as a cloak. The moment he'd seen the light, realized it came from her bedroom window, the curtains not quite closed, he'd been helpless to stop himself.

He'd always liked watching people when they didn't know he was there. He saw things they didn't want seen. He knew their dirty secrets.

Their secrets became *his* dirty little secrets.

But this was different.

The woman behind the curtains was Rory Buchanan.

He began to sweat as he neared the window even though the fall night was cold here in the mountains. The narrow shaft of light from between the curtains spilled out onto the ground. Teasing glimpses of her lured him on.

As he grew closer, he stuck the wire cutters he carried into his jacket pocket. His heart beat so hard he could barely steal a breath as he slowly stepped toward the forbidden.

The window was the perfect height. He closed his left eye, his right eye focusing on the room, on the woman.

Inside the bedroom, Rory folded a pair of jeans into one of the dresser drawers and closed the drawer, turning back toward the bed and the T-shirt she'd left lying on it.

He didn't move, didn't breathe—didn't blink as she began to disrobe.

He couldn't have moved even at gunpoint as he watched her pull the band from her ponytail, letting her chestnut hair fall to her shoulders.

She sighed, rubbing her neck with both hands, eyes closed. Wide green eyes fringed in dark lashes. He watched breathlessly as she dropped her hands to unbutton her jeans and let them drop to the floor.

Next, the Western shirt. Like her other shirts and the jackets she wore, it was too large for her, hid her body.

Anticipation had him breathing too hard. He tried to rein it in, afraid she would hear him and look toward the window. It scared him what he might do if she suddenly closed the curtains then. Or worse, saw him.

One shirt button, then another and another and the shirt fell back, dropping over her shoulders to the floor at her feet. She reached down to retrieve both items of clothing and hang them on the hook by the door before turning back in his direction.

He sucked in a breath and held it to keep from crying out. Her breasts were full and practically spilling out of the pretty pink lacy bra. The way she dressed, no one could have known.

She slid one bra strap from her shoulder, then the other. He could hear her humming now, but didn't recognize the tune. She was totally distracted. He felt himself grow hard as stone as she unhooked the bra and her breasts were suddenly freed.

A moan escaped his throat. A low keening sound filled with lust and longing. He *wanted* her, had wanted her for years, would do anything to have her…

Instinctively, he took a step toward the back of the ranch house. Rory was alone. Her house miles from any others. Her door wouldn't be locked. No one locked their doors in this part of Montana.

The sound of a vehicle engine froze him to the spot. He dropped to the ground behind the shrubs at the corner of the house as headlights bobbed through the pines. The vehicle came into view, slowed and turned around in the yard. Someone lost?

He couldn't be caught here. He hesitated only a moment before he broke for the pines behind the house and ran through the woods to where he'd hidden his car.

As he slid behind the wheel, his adrenaline waned. He'd never done more than looked. Never even contemplated more than that.

But the others hadn't been Rory Buchanan.

If that pickup hadn't come down the road when it did…

The sick odor of fear and excitement filled the car. He rolled down his window, feeling weak and powerless and angry. Tonight, he could have had her—and on his terms. *But at what cost,* he thought as he reached for the key he'd left in the ignition of the patrol car, anxious to get back to Whitehorse.

He froze. The wire cutters. He didn't feel their weight in his jacket pocket. His hand flew to the opening only to find the pocket empty.

Chapter Two

Rory Buchanan hunkered down in the dark beside the stables as six royal guards trooped past, all toting semiautomatic rifles.

To say she was in deep doo was an understatement. Not only was it now completely dark, but a storm had blown in. She felt the chill on the wind only moments before the first stinging drops of rain began to fall.

Shivering, she checked her watch. Earlier, she'd left her ranch with only a lightweight jacket, planning to return long before dark. The sky had been clear and blue, not a cloud in sight. But this was Montana, where it could snow—and did— in any month of the year.

According to her calculations the next set of guards wouldn't come past for another three minutes. Fortunately, most of the grooms and trainers had left the stables, but she could still hear someone inside with the horses.

Rory waited until the guards disappeared into the dark before she made a run for the woods.

She'd never done anything like this in her life and hated to think what her parents would have said had they still been alive. But Rory doubted her new neighbors would be trying to take her ranch if her father were around.

A duke and duchess or prince and princess—she didn't know or care which and wouldn't know a duke from a drug lord and doubted anyone else in Montana would either—had bought up all the ranches around hers.

An emissary for the royals had been trying to buy her ranch, putting pressure on her to sell. Clearly they were rich and powerful and had built a palace with all its trapping just miles from her ranch.

Rory had turned down the first few offers, saying her ranch wasn't for sale at any price. But the offers had kept coming, and just that morning she'd seen tracks again where someone had been snooping around her place.

The footprints in the dust definitely weren't hers, and since she hadn't had any male visitors for so long she couldn't remember…

She didn't even want to think about that.

Her mare was where she'd left her, hidden in the ponderosas. Retrieving her horse, Rory swung up into the saddle thinking maybe she would try to outrun the worst of the storm.

But she hadn't gone fifty yards when the sky above the pines splintered in a blinding flash of lightning followed in a heartbeat by a boom of thunder. From over by the stables, she thought for a moment she saw a dark figure standing in the shadows watching her.

Her horse shied and she had to rein in the mare to keep her seat and the mare from taking off for home. When Rory looked toward the stables again, the figure was gone. Had the person gone back inside to call the guards?

With a shudder of both cold and fear, she pulled down her cowboy hat to the storm and took off at a gallop, praying she hadn't been seen—and could get away.

Rain ran off the brim of her hat as she spurred her horse,

racing toward her ranch. She regretted that she hadn't even had the sense to grab a slicker earlier. It had been one of those beautiful fall Montana days, the stands of aspens glowing red-gold in the sunlight and the air smelling of the fallen leaves, while over the tops of the ponderosa pines, clouds floated in a sea of blue.

Lightning lit the western horizon ahead of her. She tightened the reins as thunder exploded so close it made the hair on her neck stand up. Glancing back, she could see the lights of Stanwood, a blur in the pouring rain, disappear. If she was being followed, she couldn't tell.

Suddenly being caught by armed foreign soldiers didn't seem as dangerous as trying to get to the ranch in this storm.

Better Safe Than Sorry had never been Rory Buchanan's motto. But in this case, trying to get home in the storm and darkness was crazier than even she was normally. Especially when there was an old line shack just up the mountain in a grove of aspens.

The fact that the line shack was on royal property gave her a little pause. But she valued her neck and her horse's more than she feared her neighbors at the moment. Not only was the line shack much closer than her ranch house, but also there was an old lean-to that would provide some shelter for her horse and get her out of the weather, as well.

She doubted the royal owners even knew the shack was there given the enormous amount of property they'd bought up around her. Just the thought forced a curse from her as she rode through the drowning rain and darkness to the shack.

Rory's head was still swimming with the excessiveness she'd seen only miles from her century-old ranch house. The new owners had built a palace that would rival Montana's capital. Behind it was a private airstrip, stables with an arena and a colony of small cottages and a dormitory that could house a small army—and apparently did given the number of armed soldiers she'd seen on the grounds.

Of course what had caught her eye were the horses. She'd watched a dozen grooms at least exercising the most beautiful horses she'd ever seen. She hated to think what even one of those horses might cost.

All that wealth and all these armed soldiers had her even more worried that her royal neighbors wouldn't stop until they forced her off her ranch. That and the fact that someone had definitely been snooping around her place.

She'd always felt safe on the ranch.

Until recently.

Another burst of lightning splintered the dark horizon. Thunder ricocheted through the pines. A blinding flash of lightning exposed the line shack in eerie two-dimensional relief. Rory braced herself for the thunderous boom that wasn't far behind. She hated storms worse than even the idea of spending a cold rainy night in a line shack. Her baby sister Brittany had disappeared on a night like this and just four years ago Rory's parents had been killed in a blizzard on their way back to the ranch. It had come right after she'd graduated from college and had left her with no family and a ranch to run alone.

Dismounting, she hurriedly unsaddled her horse, hobbling the mare under the lean-to and out of the downpour.

Soaked to the skin, she carried her saddle and blanket into the shack, stomping her feet on the tiny wooden porch to make sure any critters living inside would know she was coming and hopefully evacuate the premises.

The shack was about ten feet by twelve and smelled musty, but as she stepped in out of the rain, she was glad to see that there didn't seem to be anything else sharing the space with her.

It was warmer and drier inside, and she was thankful for both as she put down her saddle and slipped the still-dry horse blanket from under her arm to drop it on a worn spot on the floor next to the wall that appeared to have the least amount of dust.

Chilled, she had just started to strip off her soaked jean jacket when a flash of lightning shot through a crack in the chinking between several of the logs of the line shack, making her jump.

Outside, her horse whinnied as thunder rumbled across the mountaintop. She froze at the sound of an answering whinny from another horse nearby.

Drawing her wet jacket around her, she opened the door a crack and peered out.

A beautiful white horse with leopard spots stood in the trees below the shack. Rory caught the flash of silver from the expensive tack and saddle as lightning sliced through the darkened sky. The horse started, then bolted, taking off into the trees back the way Rory knew it had come.

She recognized the horse from earlier. A Knabstrup. She'd only read about the horses before she'd seen the groomers working with them at her royal neighbors'. Not surprising since the horses were originally from Germany—the Knabstrup breed having always been a symbol of the decadence of the aristocracy in Europe.

But where was the rider?

Rory swore as she turned back inside the shack to button her jacket and grab her hat, knowing even before she stepped into the pounding rain that the rider of the horse had been thrown and was probably lying in a puddle on the ground with his fool neck broken.

As much as she disliked storms—and the kind of neighbors who'd bought up half the county to build a palace in the middle of good pasture land that they wouldn't live in for more than a few weeks a year, if that—Rory couldn't let another human die just outside her door.

The temperature had dropped at an alarming rate, signaling an early snowstorm. Anyone left out in it was sure to freeze to death before morning.

"It would serve the danged fool right," she muttered to herself as she stomped down the mountainside to where she'd seen the horse. "Who with any common sense would go out in this kind of weather?" Unless they were trespassing on their royal neighbors' property, of course.

In a flash of lightning, she spotted the man lying in an open spot between the trees, surrounded by a bed of soft brown pine needles and a thick clump of huckleberry bushes, both of which, she hoped, had broken his fall.

She heard a groan as she neared, relieved he was alive. As he tried to sit up, she saw the blood on his forehead before the rain washed it down onto the white shirt and riding britches that he wore. He saw her and tried to struggle to his feet and failed.

"Easy," she said as she dropped down next to him on the ground.

A lock of wet black hair had tumbled over his forehead. She brushed it back to check the source of the blood and found a small cut over his left eye. There was also a goose egg rising on his temple.

Neither looked fatal.

He turned his face up to her and blinked into the driving rain. His dark hair fell back and she saw the dazed look in his very dark blue eyes. His lips turned up in a ridiculous grin as those eyes locked with hers.

"A beautiful forest sprite has come to save me?"

A forest sprite?

Clearly he was either drunk or delirious. Maybe he'd hit

his head harder than she thought. He had that odd accent like the others she'd seen at her royal neighbors'. As she leaned down to gaze into his eyes, lightning flashed around them and she was able to rule out a concussion.

"It is my lucky day, is it not?" From the smell of brandy on his warm breath and that goofy grin on his face, she'd say the man was tipsy.

Now that she saw he wasn't badly hurt and was apparently intoxicated, she took some satisfaction in the fact that he'd been thrown from his fancy mount and immediately felt guilty for the uncharitable thought.

Her teeth chattered as she glanced around for his horse, wanting nothing more than to get out of the cold and rain. His horse had apparently hightailed it back to its expensive heated stables. She couldn't blame it. She would have loved a heated stable herself just then.

A horse whinnied nearby, startling her. Not his horse. She'd seen the way it had bolted, and she doubted the horse had doubled back for the groom. Was it possible he hadn't been out riding alone? More than possible, she realized. One of the other grooms must have been with him.

"Hello?" she called through the rain and the thick darkness of the pines and descending nightfall. "You've got a groom down over here."

No answer.

She looked at the groom at her feet. He was still grinning up at her. She might have found him cute and charming and this whole incident humorous under other circumstances. Or not.

Her horse whinnied from the lean-to. This time the answering whinny was farther away. If he had been riding with someone else, they had turned back toward home, leaving him to fend for himself.

She was almost tempted to do the same thing given that the man was clearly inebriated and would now have to share her shack.

"Come on," she said cursing under her breath as she bent down to help him up. "Let's get you on your feet."

Like her, he was underdressed for this type of storm, soaking wet and shivering. She had no choice. Given his condition, he would never be able to find his way back.

"Take me to your palace beautiful forest sprite," he said and attempted a bow.

"Palace, indeed," she muttered.

Unsteady on his feet he plainly wasn't going far under his own power. He slung an arm over her shoulder. As they started up the mountainside, she wondered if he had any idea of how much trouble he was in.

He was bound to get fired for taking such an expensive horse out while drunk. He'd better hope that horse made it back to the barn safely. She'd bet that animal was worth more than this groom made in a year.

Lucky for him that he would be able to sleep it off before he had to face his boss—the duke or prince or whatever. As long as the horse returned unharmed, he might be spared being returned to his country to face a firing squad.

He shifted against her. "You are too kind, fair forest sprite."

"Aren't I, though," she grumbled. Lucky for him she couldn't let him die of hypothermia or wander off a cliff in the dark.

Lightning illuminated the landscape, the line shack appearing for an instant out of the rain and darkness. She stumbled toward the structure, staggering under the man's drunken weight as thunder boomed overhead.

"I owe you a great debt," he said as she shoved open the line shack door. "How shall I ever repay you?"

Chapter Three

Rain pounded the tin roof overhead as Rory closed the line shack door behind them. It was pitch-black in the small room except for the occasional flashes of lightning that shot through the holes in the chinking. Earsplitting booms of thunder reverberated through the shack.

Teeth chattering, Rory untangled herself from the groom and eased him to the floor beside the horse blanket. He slumped against the wall, shuddering from the cold, his eyes half-closed, making her aware of his long dark lashes—and the fact that he looked as if he was about to pass out.

Thunder rumbled overhead again, and she shivered from the cold—and her aversion to storms. She could feel the damp seeping into her bones. She was going to have to get out of her wet clothes, and quickly. So was he. And they had only the one blanket.

Fortunately, the groom looked harmless enough.

"You need to take off your wet clothing," she informed him over the pounding rain.

No response. She kicked off her boots, then started to unbutton her jeans in the dark of the cabin. She heard a thump and in a flash of lightning saw the groom had fallen over onto his side. He was curled up, shaking from the cold and apparently out like a light.

"Great." She cursed and knelt down to shake him lightly. The lashes parted, the blue behind them clearly fighting to focus on her as another shaft of light from the storm penetrated the slits between the logs. "Your clothes. They're wet," she said enunciating each syllable.

He grinned, pushed himself up and attempted to unbutton his shirt, but she saw in the flickering light from the storm that he was shivering too hard to do the job.

"Here, let me help you," she said, pushing his ice-cold fingers away to work at the buttons.

"I'm afraid my life is in your hands, my fair forest sprite." His eyelids drooped again, and she had to catch him to keep him upright.

"You *should* be afraid," she said, her own fingers trembling from the cold as she unbuttoned the dozens of tiny buttons on his fancy shirt.

As the storm raged over their heads, she pulled him forward to slip the fabric off one broad shoulder, then the other. His muscles rippled across his chest and stomach, a trail of dark curly hair dipping in a V to the waist of his riding britches.

She half turned away as she removed his britches. He slid down the wall to the floor, eyes fluttering open for a moment. Britches off, he drew the horse blanket to him, curled up and closed those blue eyes again.

Two seconds later he was snoring softly.

"Just like a man," she muttered as she stripped down to her underwear. She was chilled to the core and *he* had the horse blanket.

She stared down at the man for a moment. He had passed out, obviously having consumed more than his share of alcohol.

Outside, the storm wasn't letting up. There was little chance it would before morning. She was stuck there, and while she didn't mind sharing what little she had—the shack and her only dry horse blanket—she was piqued by the groom.

As drunk as he was, he'd had no business riding a horse, and she intended to tell him so first thing in the morning.

In the meantime… She knelt down next to him, gave him a nudge. He didn't budge. Nor did he quit snoring. Sliding under the edge of the blanket with her back to him, she shoved him over.

"Blanket hog," she muttered.

He let out a soft, unintelligible murmur, his warm breath teasing the tender skin at the back of her neck as he snuggled against her. She started to pull away, but his body felt fairly warm and definitely very solid, even the soft sound of his snoring reassuring. At least the man was good for something.

As much as she had grumbled and complained, the truth was she didn't mind having company tonight. As she began to warm up, she almost forgot about the storm raging around them as she closed her eyes and snuggled against him, drifting off to sleep.

RORY WOKE to the sound of her horse's whinny. Aware of being wonderfully warm, as if wrapped in a cocoon, the last thing she wanted to do was open her eyes.

Her horse whinnied again close by. Confused, since her horse should have been out by the barn some distance from her ranch house, she opened her eyes a slit.

Three things hit her at once.

She wasn't in her bed at the ranch.

There was an arm around her, a body snuggled behind her.

And she was *naked*.

Rory froze, listening to the man's soft, steady breathing as the events of the previous night came back in a rush. The storm, the shack, the groom she'd taken in out of the goodness of her heart.

But she was absolutely certain she had been wearing her undergarments, as skimpy as they were, when she'd lain down next to him last night. She recalled snuggling against him under the blanket to get warm…

She let out a silent curse as she recalled drowsily coming, half-awake, during the night to what she'd first thought was an erotic dream.

He stirred behind her, his warm breath tickling her bare shoulder, his arm tightening around her, one large hand cupping her left breast.

With a silent groan, it all came back, every pleasurable dreamlike moment of it, up until she'd awakened to the shock of her life.

She wasn't in the habit of waking with a stranger in her bed, let alone with a stranger on the floor of a shack under a horse blanket after having wild wanton sex.

This was all Bryce's fault. After breaking off her engagement with him four years ago, she'd been gun-shy of men. But then, who could blame her?

Blaming Bryce for this made her feel a little better. And of course there were other factors to blame: the storm, her fear of storms, the intimacy of the dark shack, the closeness of their near-naked bodies, the need for warmth to survive, Bryce again and that other need she'd ignored for obviously too long.

Not to mention trying to run the ranch single-handedly. She hadn't had time to date even though she'd had a few offers. Shoot, she'd bet everyone in the county was laying odds that she would end up a spinster. After all, she *was* nearly thirty.

Not that any of that was an excuse. She had her principles. And sleeping with a royal groom, whose name she didn't even know, didn't meet any of them.

As his breathing slowed again, signaling he'd fallen back into a deep sedated sleep, Rory slowly lifted his arm and slipped out from under it and the horse blanket. He stirred. She froze.

Then he rolled over, pulling the blanket with him, but not before she'd seen his naked backside.

She closed her eyes as she was assaulted with images of the two of them in the throes of lovemaking. A groan escaped her lips. She clamped a hand over her mouth, her eyes flying open, fearing she'd awakened him.

With relief, she saw that he was still sleeping soundly.

Her clothing was on a nail, where she'd hung it the night before. Her underwear was at the end of the horse blanket next to the groom's bare feet.

She gingerly extracted the lingerie and pulled it on. From the nail, she retrieved her shirt, which was almost dry, as were her socks. Her jeans and jean jacket were still cold and wet.

But she hardly noticed as she dressed and tried her best to ignore the hot flush of her skin or the slight whisker burn on certain parts of her body.

Don't think about it.

She wished it were that simple. She was appalled that she'd made love to a perfect stranger—and that she'd enjoyed it more than she should have.

Completely dressed, she stood for a moment telling herself maybe it *had* just been a dream. *Right.* She wasn't letting herself off that easily. Last night had been reckless, scandalous and…and…amazing. At least according to her limited experience.

As she turned to stare at the man curled in her horse

blanket, she felt almost guilty about just leaving him there to meet his fate. When she'd found him lying in the pine needles drunk and confused, she'd thought he deserved whatever punishment his royal boss would give him for riding, in an inebriated state, such a beautiful horse.

But this morning she worried that he really might be sent home to face a firing squad. She hoped that wasn't the case, but there was nothing she could do about it. In fact, since she'd refused to sell her property to his employer, it was good that no one would ever know where the groom had spent the night—or with whom.

She was grateful that he didn't know who she was. With luck, she would never see him again since the man obviously was a bad influence on her.

It dawned on her that the only two men she'd ever slept with she now had to avoid.

Not a great track record, she told herself as she picked up her saddle, eased open the door and slipped out.

DEVLIN BARROW WOKE with the worst hangover of his life. He opened his eyes to find himself wrapped in a horse blanket.

Sitting up with a start, he looked around in confusion—and alarm. He spotted his clothing draped over nails on the log walls of what appeared to be a very small cabin. But he didn't recall hanging his clothing there anymore than he could remember this place or the previous night.

The sun was up and a slight breeze blew through several cracks between the logs, chilling what he realized was his very bare skin.

"What the devil?" He rubbed his stubbled jaw and desperately tried to remember how he'd gotten there.

He had not the faintest idea. Not as to how he'd come to

be there nor where he even was. Nor could he explain his massive headache or the cut over his left eye or the tender bump he felt on his temple.

Getting shakily to his feet, he retrieved his clothing and dressed. Since he'd been wearing his riding britches and boots, he could only assume he'd gone for a ride. So where was his horse? Where was *he?*

His riding britches were cold and damp to the touch. He frowned as he remembered something. He quickly searched his pockets, only to find the first empty. In the other, he discovered a slip of paper.

The note that had been slipped under his door yesterday afternoon.

The ink had run on the paper, but he could still make out the words: *I must see you. Meet me in the aspen woods a mile to the east of Stanwood tonight after dark.*

If he'd met someone in the woods last night, he couldn't remember it.

The bump on the head, the hangover from alcohol he couldn't remember drinking and the feeling that something important had happened last night made him fear that he'd been tricked into coming to this isolated spot not to receive the news he so desperately sought, but to be…what? Killed?

He stuffed the note into his shirt pocket and, fighting a wave of nausea, opened the door and stumbled out into the sunlight. To his growing concern, he saw no sign of his horse. Nor had the horse blanket he'd been wrapped in been one from Stanwood stables.

He was becoming more concerned about the consequences of finding himself in such a predicament. He licked his lips, his mouth dry and tasting of stale brandy. Another taste teased his memory.

He shook his head as if to clear away the cobwebs and shuddered at the pain. Why was it he could remember having only one drink since he must have imbibed more than that to be feeling this awful?

Common sense told him he wouldn't have gotten drunk before his meeting in the woods. So how did he explain this headache, his lack of memory?

The thick pines outside at least told him he was in Montana, but nothing looked familiar. Not that he'd been there long enough to know his way around. Yesterday had been his first day at Stanwood.

That seemed to jar a memory. He saw himself standing in the main parlor, having a brandy with several of the nobility visiting Stanwood. He'd been called up from the stables and complimented on his riding abilities. After that, he recalled nothing.

His riding abilities? How ironic since it appeared he'd not only lost his memory—but his horse, as well.

The ground, he noted, was still wet, the pine boughs dripping bejeweled drops that caught the sunlight in blinding prisms. When had it rained? He recalled being cold, then warm.

An image flirted with his memory, but didn't stick around any longer than to make him anxious. He had to get back to Stanwood.

Taking a moment, Devlin studied the angle of the sun and started walking down the mountainside, hoping to find a road or fence or someone who could tell him where he was.

As he rubbed the knot on his temple, he chastised himself for being a fool. He'd wager he'd been tricked into riding into the storm and woods last night. As terrible as he felt, he had a feeling he was lucky to be alive.

He'd gone on a fool's errand and now he would have to pay the price. He feared it would mean his job and being sent back to his home country. He couldn't let that happen. He'd come too far, had already taken too many chances to get at the truth.

Stumbling through the woods, he headed due west. He wasn't sure how far he'd gone when he heard the thunder of hooves pounding toward him, and he looked up to see a half dozen of the royal police bearing down on him.

ALL RORY WANTED was to get back to the ranch, take a hot shower and put the storm and the groom out of her mind.

If only she could exorcize the images of the groom as easily. His lips on her skin, his strong arms around her, his hard body pressing into—

She swore as she rode out of the pines and saw the car parked in front of her ranch house.

Deputy Griffin Crowley stood against his patrol car, arms crossed over his chest, a frown on his face. He glanced at his watch as she approached, then back up at her with obvious irritation.

Rory had completely forgotten about her call to the sheriff's department yesterday morning when she'd discovered the tracks in her ranch yard. The sheriff had been unavailable. The dispatcher had promised to give someone the message though.

And here was Deputy Crowley. He'd certainly taken his sweet time getting there.

But that didn't bother her as much as the fact that she was going to have to put off the shower and dry clothing awhile longer.

"Rory," Griff said with a nod as she swung down from her saddle. He was a big man, with a head of dark blond hair and a thick mustache that curled around his thin lips. He looked like the boy next door, more boyish than handsome.

"I heard you called. The sheriff's off to some lawman's seminar in San Francisco. I got here as soon as I could. I was getting worried." He studied her openly. Almost as if he knew that she'd spent the night in the line shack with a fancy-dressed foreign groom.

She and Bryce Jones had double-dated with Griff and his girlfriend back in high school when the boys had been football stars, taking the team to state all four years. The two men had been close friends. She'd always suspected that Griff hadn't forgiven her for breaking her engagement to Bryce anymore than Bryce had.

But Griff and Bryce weren't such close friends that the deputy hadn't asked her out soon after the breakup and after Bryce's leaving town. She'd turned Griff down all four times he'd asked her out since. To her relief, he'd finally quit asking.

Unfair or not, Griff reminded her of Bryce, which was the kiss of death as far as she was concerned, not to mention she couldn't forget the way Griff had tormented her when they were kids.

"Sorry. Let me put my horse up." Needing a moment, she led her horse into the barn, slipped off the saddle and tack and hung everything in the tack room.

On the ride back to the ranch, Rory had told herself that she'd put last night behind her. It was over and done. No reason to beat herself up over it. And no one had to know about her lapse in judgment. Or whatever it had been in the middle of the night during the storm. The groom had no doubt been fired by now and was probably on his way back to whatever country he'd come from.

She filled the mare's bucket with oats before turning to find Griffin standing in the doorway watching her.

"Early morning ride?" he asked.

She knew her hair was a mess as well as her clothing, and

saw no reason to lie. "Got caught in that storm last night. I had to spend the night in an old line shack."

He raised an eyebrow. "I didn't know you had a line shack on your property."

"I don't. The one to the west was closer than trying to make it back to the ranch," she said avoiding his gaze.

Fortunately, he let it drop. "Well, at least that explains why I couldn't reach you when I called last night and again this morning," he said. "I was worried about you out here all alone after you called the department. That was a pretty bad storm last night. Temperature dropped quite a bit. I'm surprised you didn't freeze to death."

She'd always been a lousy poker player, every emotion showing in her face. "It wasn't bad in the line shack," she said, turning her whisker-burned face away.

Out of the corner of her eye, she saw him frown. "Isn't that line shack on the old Miller place? I thought that land was bought by—"

"That's the reason I called you," she cut in. "Someone has been hanging around the ranch. I think it's my new neighbors, that Duke—"

"Prince. He's a prince."

"Whatever." She just wanted to cut this short and get a hot shower and into some dry clothes. "He's been trying to buy my property and since I've made it clear I'm not selling—"

"You're telling me that the prince has been sneaking around your ranch? Come on, Rory, that's the craziest thing I've ever heard."

This was exactly why she hadn't wanted Griff responding to her call. "What are those people doing in Montana anyway? Do you even know? They could be infiltrating our country to attack us."

Griff shook his head as if he couldn't believe this. "A *prince and princess?*"

"How do you know that? Have you checked their identification? What do you actually know about these people?" She could see that he didn't know any more than she did. Maybe less since she doubted he'd been over there, while she had.

"Shouldn't someone try to find out exactly what these people are up to given they have soldiers over there carrying semiautomatic weapons?"

"How do you know what kind of weapons they carry?" he demanded.

She said nothing, not about to incriminate herself further.

Griff let out a long sigh. "First off, because they are royalty of course they are going to have armed guards. Second, you don't have to sell your land to them. Just ignore the offers."

"What about whoever's been on my property snooping around?" Rory saw his expression. "You're not going to do a thing, are you? Why am I not surprised?" She started to turn away from him, too angry to have this discussion with the pig-headed, son of a…

"Hold on, now," Griff said grabbing her arm and turning her back to face him. "I'll have a look around, okay?"

She jammed her fists on her hips and said nothing.

Apparently he seemed to think it best to follow her example and stepped past her to circle the house.

She thought about going into the house and letting him do his job, but she knew Griff. Tailing after him, she watched him wander around her ranch yard, looking bored and annoyed. He glanced back once to see if she was watching him. She was.

After a few minutes, he stopped his pretense of investigating and came back to where she was standing, her arms crossed over her chest.

"There's some tracks where someone has been hanging around, all right," he said.

"I believe I'm the one who told you that," she said, trying to contain her temper. She was cold and tired and couldn't wait for him to leave. It would be a cold day in hell before she called him out there again. Maybe when the sheriff got back…

The deputy sighed. "Look, I've been meaning to talk to you about this very thing. I don't like you living out here alone. I'm worried about you, Rory."

She shot an eyebrow upward. "Why? Since you're so sure I have nothing to worry about with my new royal neighbors…." She couldn't help the sarcasm. His concern apparently only went so far.

"Damn it, Rory, you have no business trying to run this ranch alone and this proves it. By your own admission, you got caught in that storm last night. What if you hadn't been able to get to the line shack? Or worse—what if you'd gotten bucked off your horse and hurt?"

She bristled. "I'm *fine*."

Griffin was shaking his head. "I'm not sure you can trust your judgment on this. You aren't behaving rationally, and you know it."

If he only knew. "If you're going to tell me you think I should sell the ranch—"

"You know you're doing this out of sheer stubbornness. It would be different if you had a man around—"

"I'm in no mood for this."

"I can see that you didn't get much sleep last night," he said. "Maybe this isn't the best time to bring this up."

"There is no good time if this is about me getting rid of the ranch," she said with heat although she knew others in town had speculated on the same thing—if not bet on how long before she ran the place into the ground. What Griffin and everyone else didn't seem to understand was that she loved the ranch and couldn't bear to part with it.

Just this year, she'd sold off the cattle and leased the land, telling herself it was only temporary, just until she could get the ranch back in business.

"I'm not selling." With that she turned and stomped toward the house.

"I wasn't offering to *buy* the place," Griff called after her. "I was asking you to *marry* me."

Rory stumbled to a halt, his words pelting her like stones. Slowly she turned to look back at him.

"What?" she asked, telling herself she must have heard wrong. She'd turned him down for even a date. What would make him think she would marry him?

"We should get married." He walked to her, kneading the brim of his hat in his fingers nervously as he approached. "I'd planned to ask you a lot better than this, but when you weren't around this morning... I'm asking you to marry me."

Her first indication was to laugh, but the deputy looked so serious... "Griff, I don't know what to say." That was putting it mildly.

"I know this is probably a little unexpected."

You think?

"But I've been considering it for some time," he continued, clearly nervous. "You need a man out here. You can't run the place by yourself."

She bristled at that. "Even if that were true, it's no reason to get married," she said, still stunned by his proposal.

"Hell, Rory, people get married every day with a whole lot less in common than the two of us. You and I have known each other all our lives. There shouldn't be any surprises."

Yeah, who'd want any surprises in a marriage? Or mystery? Or excitement? Or, say…love?

"Griff, I appreciate the offer, but I believe people should be in love when they get married. I don't love you." She hardly liked him after the way he used to tease and taunt her when they were kids.

"Love?" He snorted. "Like you're one of those silly romantic types."

"I beg your pardon?"

"Come on, Rory. Look at you. The way you dress. The way you act. Hell, if someone saw you out in the pasture they'd take you for a cowhand rather than a woman." He sounded angry with her.

For a moment, she was too shocked to speak. She might be a tomboy, but that didn't mean she wasn't a woman under these clothes. She had a right to romance, love, passion. A red-hot memory of last night in the shack leaped into her thoughts against her will. Talk about passion…

"You know what I mean," he said, softening his words. "You've never acted like a woman."

"If there is a compliment in there, I'm afraid I missed it," she said, fire in her eyes.

"What are you getting all riled about?" Griff demanded. "I was just saying that you could do a whole lot worse than me."

"I think you've said enough, Griff."

"I didn't mean to offend you."

"I'm not offended." She was. Not that everything he'd said wasn't the truth. Obviously, she didn't dress or act much like his idea of a woman. But under her damp dirty clothes, there was a woman's body and a beating heart.

Her thoughts flashed to the groom she'd shared her horse blanket—and a lot more—with last night. He'd found her desirable, hadn't he? True, he'd been drunk as a skunk and thought she was a forest sprite.

"Well, at least consider my offer," Griff said irritably. "I'll give you some time to think about it. But I could be the answer to your problems."

"I don't have any problems," she snapped. Except Griff right then. "You and I are *friends*." A lie. "Let's leave it at that."

"*Friends* isn't a bad place to begin a marriage."

"My answer is no," she said more forcefully.

"You are one mule-headed woman, you know that?"

"Thank you. That's the nicest thing you've said to me this morning." She turned again and headed for the house, calling over her shoulder, "Let me know about what you find out about my new neighbors."

Once inside the house, the front door locked behind her, Rory waited until Griff drove away before she stripped off her damp clothing and stepped into the shower, hopping mad. Griff had caught her off guard with his ridiculous marriage proposal. But it was his description of her that had her fuming because she feared it was too close to the truth.

She'd been so involved in saving the ranch that maybe she had forgotten how to be a woman.

Until last night.

Chapter Four

With dread, Devlin watched the horsemen approach. Jules Armitage, the head of royal security, rode in the lead, his back ramrod straight.

Devlin heard Armitage referred to as "Little Napoleon" behind his back. Small in stature but with an air of importance because of his long-standing position with the royal family, Jules was a man easily ridiculed.

But Devlin knew Jules Armitage was also a man to be feared. Jules had been in the service of the royal family for thirty years. His loyalties were never questioned, his harsh dealings with those under him legendary.

Devlin had seen Jules take a horse whip to one groom. Another groom had simply disappeared. The head of security had free rein here in Montana. Anything could fall under the protecting of the only daughter of the king, including murder.

Devlin could see even from a distance that the head of security was furious. It showed in the set of his shoulders, in the way he forced his horse's head up. Jules would report this incident—if he hadn't already.

This was the worst thing that could happen. Devlin couldn't be sent home now, and yet he knew the princess could do whatever she wanted with him. He was at her whim. As were the rest of those under her rule here at Stanwood.

With a wave of his hand, the head of security ordered the other riders to hold back. Jules rode on alone, bringing his horse to an abrupt halt within a few feet of Devlin.

His horse danced to one side as Jules dismounted with a curse that could have been directed at the horse—or at the groom.

Back still stiff, his reproach barely contained, Jules turned to face him. "Lord Ashford requests your presence in the stables at once," he said, voice taut with fury.

Devlin expected a tongue-lashing at the very least. This reaction was all wrong. "Lord Ashford?" he repeated, his aching head adding to his confusion.

Jules's complexion darkened. "I suggest you ride directly to the Stanwood stables. His lordship is *waiting*." The little man held out his reins with a stiff arm, and Devlin realized Jules was furious at being sent on such an errand let alone being forced to give up his horse in doing so.

While Jules could do little about Lord Ashford, he could definitely make Devlin's life hell—and his look promised as much.

Without a word, Devlin took the reins and swung up into the saddle. His head swam and he had to steady himself for a moment before he spurred the horse and took off at a gallop toward the stables.

As Stanwood came into view, Devlin thought, as he had the first time he'd seen it yesterday, it was amazing what too much wealth and self-indulgence could do when let loose.

Stanwood, a miniature of the royal palace in their home-land, rose out of the pines, a massive palace of quarried stone. One second-floor wing housed the princess and her prince, while the other wing was for royal guests.

Behind the palace were the stables, corrals and arena. Tucked back into the mountainside in the trees were a dozen small cottages that had been built for the grooms and horse trainers. Servants quarters had been erected in the opposite direction for those who saw to the princess and her entourage's daily needs as well as those of visiting nobility.

As he stepped into the stables, Devlin found Lord Nicholas Ashford, one such guest, leaning against a stall door. One glance around told him that the building was empty except for Lord Ashford. This, he knew, was no accident.

Lord Nicholas Ashford was tall, slim and immaculately groomed as any in his social stratosphere. Like the other nobles Devlin had come in contact with, Ashford had an air of privilege about him and an underlying impatience; he was easily bored. And he was a man who didn't like being kept waiting.

Nicholas frowned when he saw him. "You look like hell."

"I feel worse," Devlin said. He glanced around. Even though the stables appeared empty, he always feared that someone was close by, listening. Royal gossip was a hot commodity.

"We're alone. I cleared everyone out." Nicholas smiled. He'd never made it a secret that he enjoyed the privileges that came with wealth and power. His smile waned, though, as he studied Devlin.

"I feared something had happened when I heard your horse returned last night without you. Apparently there was cause for concern," he said, eyeing the knot on Devlin's temple. "What the devil happened?"

"It seems I was unseated from my horse."

Nicholas scoffed. "You? Not likely."

Devlin had practically grown up on the back of a horse. The last time he recalled being thrown was when he was five. "I have no memory of it."

"The head wound doesn't appear that serious," Nicholas noted.

"It's not. I fear it was the brandy I had before I left Stanwood. I suspect it was drugged." How else could he explain ending up in that cabin with the unfamiliar horse blanket and no memory of what had happened the entire night?

"Drugged, you say?" Nicholas didn't seem surprised. "There's something you might want to see."

Nicholas, he realized, had been waiting for him at the stall containing the horse Devlin had ridden out into the woods last night. The horse that had returned without him.

"Take a look at his right hind quarter," Nicholas said as Devlin opened the stall door. The mount shied away from him, eyes wild, nostrils flaring.

Devlin felt his senses go on alert. The horse hadn't behaved in this manner when he'd ridden him away from Stanwood last night. Even when the storm had come in, the horse hadn't reacted to the thunder and lightning because it had been trained to be ridden by hunters, who would be shooting while riding.

Speaking in a low soothing voice, Devlin cautiously entered the stall. The horse relaxed some as Devlin continued to gentle it with his words and slow, measured movements. Gingerly, he ran his hand the length of the animal and felt something. The gelding shied away from him again.

"Easy, boy." He found the spot Nicholas had mentioned. Something had penetrated the hide, leaving a small hole. It wasn't deep, hadn't come from a bullet.

He glanced at Nicholas, who nodded. "Shot with, if I had to guess, a pellet gun. You do recall that old pellet gun we used to get in trouble with?"

Devlin did indeed. Their friendship had been a secret. The son of a stables owner and the son of a noble. Nicholas, who'd been skinny and pale, had been sent to the stables to learn to ride. They'd been close in age, Devlin strong and fearless, Nicholas puny and timid.

The friendship had been good for both of them. Nicholas had learned to ride a horse, as well as take part in rough-and-tumble adventures with Devlin. And in turn, Devlin had learned the speech and manners of a noble.

"I think we can assume that someone knows why you're here," Nicholas said, concern in his tone.

"It would appear so." Devlin took out the note that had been slipped under his door at his cottage. "You didn't send this, then?"

Nicholas took the piece of paper, squinting in the poor light at the water-blurred writing.

"I don't recognize the handwriting, but whoever sent it either appeared to be in a hurry or purposely scrawled the note so as to remain anonymous," he said, handing it back.

"I thought it might have been from you. Or Anna," he added quietly. His mother's housemaid and friend had been an excellent horsewoman.

"Dev, I was as fond of your mother as my own, but even if you find out who murdered her, it won't bring her back and will only succeed in getting you killed, as well. I was opposed to this from the beginning, but now that someone knows why you're here…" Nicholas stopped as he must have realized he was wasting his breath.

They'd had this conversation before and always with the same outcome. Devlin had to know not only who had murdered his mother but also why. It made no sense. His only lead was the woman who'd found his mother's body—his mother's housemaid and friend. Anna Pickering had been in the house. She would know if the rumor he'd heard was true—that a royal soldier had been seen leaving the house that night shortly before his mother's body was discovered.

It made no sense to kill a woman who owned a stable, who wasn't politically motivated and who had always catered to royalty.

"If you're right about Anna seeing the murderer that night, she won't want to see you," Nicholas said.

Devlin didn't blame the woman. She had disappeared right after the murder. Nicholas had helped Devlin trace her to the princess's new palace in Montana—and had helped Devlin get hired as a groom there.

"Do you remember who handled your drink last night?" Nicholas asked. "I'm afraid I didn't notice."

Devlin had replayed the scene in his mind. He'd been given a brandy in the main parlor of Stanwood, surrounded by the noble class.

Nicholas had instigated the whole thing as a way to get Devlin into Stanwood so he could check out the layout of the place. He'd introduced him as a master horseman, touted his skills at training horses and riders alike, himself included, and made sure everyone understood his kinship with the groom and respected it.

Of course, that wouldn't save Devlin if the princess found out what he was really up to.

"The longer you stay here, the more dangerous it will become," Nicholas said now. "Perhaps I should try to speak with this woman, Anna Pickering. You say she is a handmaid for the princess?"

"You have done enough." Nicholas had already stuck his neck out far enough just helping him get the groom job—and getting him access to Stanwood last night.

"If anyone can persuade her to meet you, it's me," Nicholas said with a grin.

"And should she tell Princess Evangeline what you have done?"

"I shall deny it, of course." Nicholas laughed. "Just as I shall deny any knowledge of your deception when you get caught."

"Of course," Devlin said, but knew better. He feared Nicholas would put himself in danger to save his friend.

That was why he had to protect Nicholas—and Anna—at all costs.

"Watch your back around Jules Armitage," Devlin warned his friend.

"Don't worry about the Little Napoleon. I can handle him."

Devlin didn't doubt it, but he'd seen how upset Jules had been. The head of security didn't like being treated like an errand boy. He wouldn't forget this slight. Nor who had caused it.

After saddling a horse for Nicholas, as if that had been why Lord Ashford had ordered him to the stables, Devlin headed for his cottage to shower and change.

Last night was still a black hole. Worse, he couldn't shake the feeling that it was imperative that he remember. There was little doubt that he'd been lured into the woods, drugged and meant to lose his horse, but for what purpose?

Had his attacker hoped the fall from the horse would kill him? Or had his attacker planned to finish him off but hadn't for some reason?

He was almost to his cottage when he had a sudden vision. Hot skin, silken and flushed with heat, full rounded breasts, nipples erect and thighs as creamy as… He stumbled in surprise.

Being drugged and thrown from his horse had done more than left him with a raging headache. It had apparently played hell with his dreams last night.

RESTLESS AFTER CHORES, Rory stormed into the house and went straight to her bedroom and the antique full-length mirror that had belonged to her grandmother.

Her face was flushed from the cold morning, tendrils of her chestnut hair curled around her face from where they'd escaped from her ponytail. Her Western jacket and flannel Western shirt had been her father's. She hadn't been able to part with either of them. The jacket was worn and too big for her, but like the shirt, it was soft and comfortable and one of her favorites.

Her jeans were boot-cut, slim-fit but the large shirt and jacket she wore over them pretty much hid her figure.

She cocked her head, shoved back her Western straw hat and studied her face in the mirror. No makeup. She'd bought some lip gloss recently, but she didn't know where she'd put it. As for mascara, well, she hadn't worn any since…her high school prom? Had it really been over ten years ago?

Rory groaned. Griff was right. She looked like a cowhand. She'd always preferred working outside with her father rather than being in the kitchen cooking with her mother.

Even now, if she wasn't on a horse, then she'd just as soon be out mending fences. Because of that, she was a mediocre cook, could bake if forced to, and her sewing abilities extended to reinforcing a button.

She much preferred jeans and boots to dresses and had never owned a pair of high heels. She'd borrowed a pair of her mother's for the high school prom—and had kicked them off the moment she'd gotten to the dance.

Damn Griffin Crowley. Tears smarted her eyes. She brushed angrily at them. It made it all the worse that Griff of all people was right, she thought as she stalked into the kitchen and dug out her mother's recipe book.

Damn if she wouldn't cook something.

It would keep her mind off last night and the groom who'd awakened something in her that she realized had been asleep. Or in a coma.

HEAD OF SECURITY Jules Armitage watched the small jet taxi to a stop on the airstrip behind Stanwood. Lord Charles Langston emerged from the craft.

A steady flow of guests had been arriving for several days, no doubt to attend the masquerade ball the princess had planned for this coming Saturday.

But still, it seemed odd that the royal family barrister would be invited to the ball. More than likely, Princess Evangeline had sent for him on a legal matter.

Jules knew the princess felt slighted because being born female exempted her from the throne in their home country. Nor could her husband, merely a lord before he married the princess, take the throne upon her father's death.

But Prince Broderick would be elevated to a high position within the country should the king die. That was part of the reason for the unrest in their home country. Few people wanted to see Prince Broderick Windham having anything to do with the running of their country.

It was one reason Jules suspected that the princess and her husband had been sent to Montana. While the princess had overseen the construction of Stanwood since the first shovel of dirt had been turned over, she clearly hadn't been happy about her apparent exile.

Her husband, Prince Broderick, had been in charge of buying up as many ranches as possible for their new home.

Jules questioned this entire move. While he could understand the king's reasoning, since both Princess Evangeline and Prince Broderick were definite liabilities in their homeland, Jules had to wonder, why the U.S.—let alone Montana?

If the king hoped that Montana would change his son-in-law and perhaps keep him at home long enough to produce an heir, His Royal Highness would have been sorely disappointed had he known the truth.

Jules swore as a second person stepped from the plane onto the tarmac. Lady Monique Gray, a recent widow. Black widow, that was.

What was *she* doing here? As if Jules had to ask. The princess's husband. Broderick had been anything but discreet about his scandalous affair with the woman. If the king hadn't controlled the media, it would have been all over the news. Princess Evangeline had to have heard about it, even though her father had worked so hard to keep it from her.

What the king didn't know was that his precious princess was a lot less fragile than he thought. She could squash a black widow like Lady Monique Gray—and would if given half a mind to. Lady Gray might not realize it yet, but she'd made a mistake coming here. Here in Montana, Princess Evangeline ruled like her father. If there wasn't blood shed within a fortnight, Jules would be surprised.

"Royals," he muttered under his breath, then quickly turned to make sure no one had overheard. In Stanwood, the walls had ears and unless he wanted to lose his, he'd best watch himself. The king had personally put him in charge of the princess's safety. Not that she needed it. Instead, he would probably find himself trying to protect the others from her.

He found the whole lot of them tiresome. Especially the lords and ladies who hung around the princess like flies to spoiled meat. Lord Nicholas Ashford came to mind. Jules hated beginning the day by being sent like a messenger boy to find a missing groom.

Especially this particular groom.

Princess Evangeline had asked him to keep an eye on Devlin Barrow and make sure he had everything he needed, including a cottage of his own near the stables and the run of the place. Jules suspected she planned to take him as a lover. What other reason could she have for singling out the groom?

Jules had done as ordered, but there'd been a breach in security just before dark last evening and he'd lost track of the groom. Someone had been seen on the property, sneaking around. That had taken his attention and the next thing he'd known Devlin Barrow had disappeared, last seen riding off into the rain and darkness.

It wasn't until that morning that Jules had been informed that a horse had returned without a rider—and that not all of the hired help had been accounted for. Devlin Barrow hadn't returned.

Jules had barely gotten that news when Lord Nicholas Ashford had demanded that the head of security not only find Devlin, but bring him at once to the stables.

Given no choice, since he was subordinate to every guest of the princess's, Jules had done as ordered.

But it had stuck in his craw. Why had the groom ridden off so late last night and in a storm? And where had he spent the night after losing his horse?

If Lord Ashford hadn't ordered his favorite groom be found

for his morning ride, Jules would have given the groom more than the tongue-lashing he deserved. Within reason, he thought, as he reminded himself that Devlin Barrow was to receive special treatment. Wasn't it always the troublemakers who curried the nobles' favor?

But why this particular groom?

Jules knew he should just let it go. Who cared what had happened to the groom last night? The princess hadn't found out. Better it be forgotten.

But Jules couldn't let it go. As head of security, he was going to find out not only what Devlin Barrow had been up to last night, but also why the son of a stables owner was suddenly being afforded such special treatment.

Picking up the phone, Jules called down to the stables. "Ready me a horse. No, I'll be going alone."

PRINCESS EVANGELINE Stanwood Wycliffe Windham studied herself in the full-length mirror. Behind her back, she knew people tsk-tsked about how sad it was that she'd taken after her mother's side of the family instead of her father's. The king was quite good-looking, while her mother, rest her soul, had been average.

Evangeline herself was below average. While she was average height, slim enough, blessed with her father's dark hair and dark blue eyes, her facial features would have been more attractive on a horse than a woman.

She knew she was being too critical. She had what once would have been called *handsome* features. Strong, striking bone structure. And she carried it off with a regal air that had definitely made some men turn their heads.

But then again, she was *the* princess. She knew that was why Broderick had pursued her. He'd wanted the title, the wealth, the prominence. He'd been so handsome, so charming and so attentive that she'd overlooked his less favorable qualities and married him because she thought they'd produce beautiful heirs to the throne.

Evangeline snorted and spun away from the mirror to stare out the window. "Bastard," she spat out at the thought of her philandering husband. She could overlook his infidelities and had. But his latest offense was unforgivable.

The bastard hadn't given her an heir and now he wasn't even sharing her bed. Maybe he thought he'd outlive her and have a chance to rule. Once her father was dead.

Her father. Just the thought of him made her a little ill. She knew he found her a scheming wench. He had no idea, she thought, then warned herself to tread carefully. She had taken too many liberties as it was. She'd disappointed her father too many times.

Her failure to produce a male heir, any heir at all, had angered him. He blamed her even though Lord Broderick Windham had given her little choice. Broderick, it seemed, was her punishment for her sins.

And sins, she had many. Her latest, though, was the most dangerous. She knew if she crossed her father that she risked not only being exiled from her homeland indefinitely, but also losing her freedom, possibly even her life.

Not that she didn't have everything under control. She reminded herself how clever she'd been when Lord Nicholas Ashford had come to her with his request that she hire Devlin Barrow as a groom at her new home in Montana.

It was clear to her that while Devlin had gone into hiding and no one had been able to find him after his mother's murder, Lord Nicholas was in contact with him.

Evangeline had provided the bait—Anna Pickering—by

bringing the woman to Montana on the pretense of protecting her. Everything had worked just as she'd planned it.

So far.

But Evangeline could feel time slipping through her fingers like the finest sand. It was a two-edged sword, keeping both Anna Pickering and Devlin Barrow safe while at the same time planning their destruction.

Evangeline let out an un-princesslike curse as she focused on the scene below her window.

"What is Monique doing here?" her companion Laurencia cried as she joined the princess at the window.

Evangeline spun away from the window as the Black Widow entered Stanwood.

"You don't think *Broderick* invited her, do you?" Laurencia asked wide-eyed.

"Of course not," Evangeline snapped sarcastically. It was so like her friend to say the obvious. Who else could have invited her? Lady Monique was relentless once she set her sights on a man. And now apparently she'd set her sights on the prince. And vice versa.

This was the last straw. Evangeline had put up with her husband's philandering for the last time. The fool was going to produce a bastard who would try to overthrow the crown one day. Evangeline had to get pregnant, and soon, to put an end to the talk of her being barren.

But that would mean getting her husband into their marital bed. That, she knew, would take more than fortitude on her part, due to his complete lack of interest—and her own.

It would take a miracle.

Or something Princess Evangeline was better equipped for: deception.

"You should have Lady Monique sent from the grounds at

once," Laurencia was saying. "She is only here to rub your face in her affair with your husband."

Thank you, Laurencia, Evangeline thought. That was the problem with having a stupid companion—while she could be useful, she was annoyingly clueless.

"We will welcome Monique," Evangeline said as she suddenly saw Lady Monique's arrival as a possible godsend.

"But I thought—"

"Best let me do the thinking," she told her. Laurencia had always been the perfect companion—meek and slow-witted and completely loyal. In short, Evangeline could wrap her around her little finger.

"I want you to be nice to Monique," the princess said. "She has arrived just in time for the masquerade ball. In fact, I want you to make sure she wears the costume *you* were planning to wear. I shall have the seamstress make you something more suitable."

Laurencia looked disappointed but nodded.

Evangeline smiled. Her original plan had been to use her companion to lure in Lord Prince Broderick by offering Laurencia on a silver platter. But this new plan would work much better since she had been dangling Laurencia in front of her husband for weeks and he hadn't gone for the bait.

With Monique, the Black Widow, there would be no need to dangle her. Instead, Evangeline would have to make sure Broderick was kept so busy he wouldn't have the time to catch Monique—until the night of the masquerade ball.

With everyone masked, it would be the time to spring her trap and produce an heir to the throne. Broderick, without realizing it, would do his part. Once she was pregnant with a legitimate heir…well, then she wouldn't need Broderick anymore, would she?

Montana was such a wild, isolated country. Anything could happen to a man as adventurous as Prince Broderick Windham. Most certainly a very painful death.

Evangeline glanced at her watch. "Off with you now to make sure Lady Monique is comfortable in the large suite on the east wing." Laurencia, who as always did as she was told, scampered off to do the princess's bidding.

The princess stepped to the window again, pleased with herself. A lone rider galloped across the meadow.

Jules? Riding off alone? Odd, she thought, but quickly returned her thoughts to a more important task. Tying up one last loose end.

At the sound of a knock on her suite door, Princess Evangeline glanced at her watch. The man was prompt, she thought as she opened the door to her second cousin by marriage, Lord Charles Langston, the family barrister from a noble but poor family.

"Your Royal Highness," Lord Charles said with a bow. He looked scared out of his wits. She considered that a very good sign as she ushered him into the room, closed the door and demanded to see what he'd brought her.

Holding her breath, she watched him reach into his briefcase and draw out a large manila envelope. What Charles carried was of such high security that if caught with the papers, he would have been put to death.

Her fingers shook as she took the envelope and drew out the papers, noting not only the royal seal, but the thick, pale green paper used only for important government documents in her country.

"These are the originals?" she asked.

Charles nodded.

"So it is true," she said, feeling sick to her stomach. There would be no turning back now. She put the documents back into the manila envelope, willing her fingers not to tremble at even the thought of what she'd done.

Finally, she looked to the family barrister. She feigned surprise, then anger. "Where is this bastard?"

"In your employ, your Royal Highness. He's one of your grooms."

JULES RODE TO THE SPOT where he'd encountered Devlin Barrow that morning. The day was cold and clear, the sun slicing through the tall, dense pines. Plenty of light to track Devlin's footprints in the still-wet ground.

Determined to find out where the groom had spent the night, he followed the trail, glad for last night's rain, which made tracking easier.

A hawk squawked as it circled over the treetops. Closer, a squirrel chattered at him as he worked his way through the pines.

Jules lost the tracks at one point in the thick, dried pine needles but picked them up again as he led his horse up the mountainside, surprised the groom had ridden this far from the ranch. He could make out the old county road—all that stood between the princess's property and the one ranch that was still privately owned.

The owner had refused to sell. He'd heard Evangeline discussing the problem with her husband, Prince Broderick. The Buchanan Ranch was now all that stood between the prince's holdings and the river.

The owner would *have* to sell. It was only a matter of time since the princess wanted it—and Broderick was responsible for acquiring the property for her.

Jules turned his attention back to the mountainside and the boot tracks he'd been following. As he walked through a stand of aspens, the leaves golden, he saw the small log structure ahead.

The groom's boot tracks led right up to the front door. Was it possible this was where Devlin Barrow had spent the night?

Ground-tying his horse, Jules walked toward the shack, noting the shed roof off to one side. A horse had been kept under the overhang recently. He could still smell it.

Not the groom's horse since it had returned to the stables without him. Had Devlin been thrown? That would explain his odd behavior that morning as well as the wound on his temple.

Except that Devlin Barrow was extolled as being an extraordinary horseman.

To Jules's surprise, the door to the structure wasn't locked. Cautiously he peered inside, not sure what he expected to find.

That was just it. He hadn't expected to find *anything*. It took a moment for his eyes to adjust to the darkness—and see the horse blanket lying on the shack's worn wood floor.

Frowning, he stepped in for a closer look. The horse blanket wasn't one of Stanwood's, which were monogrammed with the royal crest.

He caught a scent in the stale air of the small room and smiled knowingly. A man who knew about the baser desires, Jules was familiar with the aroma of sex.

He stared down at the blanket, wondering who had shared that blanket with the groom last night and how he could use that knowledge to his advantage.

Obviously, the woman wasn't from the Stanwood household or she would have been riding one of the royal horses with the monogrammed blanket and tack.

So who was she?

He started to turn to leave when he saw something that stopped him. Crouching down, he lifted the edge of the horse blanket. It had appeared to be nothing more than cheap material like most blankets used under a Western saddle in this part of the world.

But this blanket had leather trim. It was what had been stamped into the leather that caught his eye. Whitehorse Days.

Jules frowned as he read the date and the words: All-around Best Cowgirl.

He dropped the blanket back to where he'd found it and rose. All-around Best Cowgirl. She shouldn't be that hard to find given that he now had the event date.

If Devlin Barrow—or even the princess—thought either of them could keep secrets from him, they were both mistaken.

Chapter Five

"What is *that?*" Georgia Michaels asked as she answered the door to find her best friend standing on her step.

Rory held out the dish as an offering. "Pie. Apple. I baked it."

Georgia looked suspiciously from Rory to the pie and back but didn't take it. "You're kidding."

"No. Take the damned thing. Why is everyone giving me such a hard time about this?" Rory said, shoving the pie at her friend.

Georgia took the pie, eyeing her warily, before leading the way into the house. "Who's giving you a hard time about this pie?" she asked on the way to her warm, sunny kitchen.

"Deputy Griffin Crowley. And not about the pie," Rory said with a groan as she climbed onto a stool at the breakfast bar. "He asked me to marry him."

"Get out of here." Georgia laughed as she found a knife, cut the pie and dished them up each a slice, still eyeing the pie with suspicion.

"He called his proposal an *offer* and made it sound like a business proposition."

"*Romantic.*" Georgia took a tentative bite of the pie, her expression turning to one of surprise. "Hey, this is *good.*"

Rory cut her eyes to her. "Don't sound so shocked. I can bake. If I want to."

"Did Griff say you couldn't bake? Is that what this is about?"

"He insinuated that I wasn't a real woman."

Georgia raised an eyebrow.

"He actually made fun of me when I told him I didn't want to marry anyone I didn't love, then he pointed out that I wasn't much of a *girl*."

Her friend laughed. "I remember when you punched Joey Franklin in the mouth in third grade because he called you a girl. You can't have it both ways."

Rory had to laugh as well. "I know."

"So what did you tell him?" she asked and took another bite of the pie.

"I told him no, of course. He said he only suggested it because I need help with the ranch. I think I hurt his feelings. He got pretty angry."

Georgia kept her gaze on the pie in front of her. "You do need help out there. What are you going to do?"

"I don't know." Rory didn't have money to hire hands and the place was getting rundown without an infusion of cash. She couldn't afford to ranch. And she couldn't afford not to since ranching was her life.

"Have you given any more thought to my offer?" Georgia asked cautiously. Her friend wanted her to come into the knitting shop as a business partner even though attempts to teach Rory to knit had failed miserably.

"I'd die without the ranch," Rory said dramatically. "Or at least I'd want to. And as for selling out to royalty…" She shook her head. "I hate that they bought up so many working ranches to build some monstrosity. You know they'll tire of it and go back to wherever they came from. Or just visit here a few months a year after ruining all that range land."

"Nice to see you getting along so well with your new neighbors. Can I assume you didn't take *them* a pie?"

Rory let out a curse that made her friend laugh. "But I did meet one of the grooms from the place."

"Oh?" Georgia's head came up, eyes gleaming. She knew Rory too well.

"We both got caught in that big storm that blew through last night," Rory said, picking up her fork and poking at her piece of pie. She still hadn't taken a bite.

"And?"

Rory wished she hadn't mentioned it. But Georgia was her best friend and had been since they were knee-high to a squirrel. And Rory couldn't just bake a pie and show up on her best friend's doorstep and not confide all.

"And…we might have made love," she blurted.

"Might have? You don't *know?"*

Rory felt her face grow warm. "I'm pretty sure we did."

"It couldn't have been very memorable."

"Actually…" She looked away, her face now flaming.

"Rory!" Georgia laughed. "Does this mean you aren't joining the nunnery like everyone in town has been saying since your breakup with Bryce?"

"Not funny."

"So when are you seeing him again?"

"I'm not."

"What?" Georgia didn't even bother to hide her disappointment.

"Even if he didn't work for my royal-pain-in-the-behind neighbors, I'm pretty sure he got fired after last night." She wasn't about to admit that she'd been thinking of riding back over there that afternoon, get close enough that she could see the grooms exercising the horses to see if he was all right.

She doubted he remembered last night as out of it as he'd been. But it would be nice to know he hadn't been sent back to his country to be executed for risking one of the horses.

"You haven't touched your pie," her friend noted suspiciously again.

"I haven't been hungry all day. I feel like I'm coming down with something."

"Nothing kills my hunger," Georgia said proudly and finished her piece of pie. "Except love." Her eyes shone as she grinned at Rory. "Maybe you're in love."

"Please. I don't even know the man's name and I can assure you what happened last night wasn't love. It was more like lust. A lot like lust."

"Or fate. Apparently this royal *groom* thought you were a woman," Georgia said hiking up one eyebrow. "You should have told Griffin Crowley that!"

Rory laughed, glad she'd come to see her friend, glad she'd confided in her. Georgia always made her feel better. "Thank you. Talking about last night, well, I feel better."

"I suppose this means no more pies, then," Georgia joked.

Talking about last night, though… Rory let out a curse and jumped to her feet. "My horse blanket."

"What?" Georgia looked alarmed.

"I left my horse blanket in the line shack. The groom was still sleeping on it so I left it."

"So it's probably still there," her friend said reasonably. "Or you can replace it, right?"

"You don't understand. I just remembered. It was the horse blanket I won at Whitehorse Days in high school."

"That old thing?"

"Georgia, the date of the event, Whitehorse Days and Best All-around Cowgirl were imprinted on the leather trim."

Her friend's eyes widened. "So he'll find you. What's wrong with that?"

"I told you, he is probably on his way back to his country right now." Rory had to get the blanket back. She was sure it was still in the shack. The blanket was old and certainly not a keepsake since Rory had won her share of horse blankets over the years. But she didn't want anyone else to find it and trace it back to her.

The last thing she needed was for her royal neighbors to find out she'd been trespassing on their property.

DEVLIN HAD GOTTEN CALLED BACK to the stables to saddle more horses for the royal guests.

Hours later, he finally reached his cottage. Now, standing under the spray of the shower, he closed his eyes. His head still ached, but he felt a little stronger. He'd tried to remember who'd poured him the brandy last night. It could have been anyone, one of the servants or one of the aristocrats who'd been in the room.

He'd tried to picture where everyone had been as he'd entered. Princess Evangeline Windham had been sitting on the couch. Her husband, Prince Broderick, had been standing before the fireplace, a drink already in his hand.

Nicholas had been talking to Lady Laurencia Hurst, a mousy-looking woman with timid brown eyes. Lord Alexis Kent had been behind Evangeline. A pretty boy, Alexis had been the lover of a variety of royal women, including Evangeline herself, at least according to Nicholas, and Nicholas did love royal gossip.

None of them had looked as if they were a crack shot

with a pellet gun, but looks could be deceiving, Devlin knew only too well.

He had been introduced by Nicholas as his favorite groom from the famous Barrow Stables.

"He comes highly recommended," Nicholas had said.

"Here, here," said Prince Broderick. "Your mother trained some of our horses. A fine, talented woman." Some of King Wycliffe's horses, not the Windhams', Devlin had thought. Broderick's family had been at the low end of nobility.

"Devlin's mother is recently deceased," Nicholas had added.

"Oh?" Broderick had seemed genuinely surprised to hear that. "My condolences. Get the man a drink," he'd said to the servant at the bar.

Then Princess Evangeline had insisted Devlin have a seat in front of the fire next to her and tell her how she could improve her riding skills.

All Devlin remembered was someone thrusting a glass into his hand. As darkness had descended, he'd excused himself and hurried to the stables, anxious to reach the stand of aspens and his appointment.

Had someone left the group in the main parlor and followed him through the rain and darkness? Or was the person who'd sent him on the wild goose chase not of royal class? And the person who shot his horse, an accomplice? Perhaps a servant? Or a royal soldier?

Devlin closed his eyes and concentrated on the feel of the hot water pelting his body. The images came in a rush, hitting him harder than the water, bombarding him with visions of a woman with green eyes, long legs and—

His eyes flew open, the images were so real he'd half expected to find the woman in his arms. Disappointment and confusion made his head swim.

He leaned against the shower wall for a moment, wondering if he was losing his mind or if it had just been the drug he'd been given. But the images were so vivid, so defined, so powerful…

How was it possible that he could remember the feel of the woman's skin beneath his fingertips, the weight of her breasts cupped in his palms, the sound of her quickened breathing if it had only been a dream?

Because it *hadn't* been a dream.

He shut off the water, his head clearing a little. What if he hadn't been alone last night?

It was the only explanation for the taunting images of this illusive green-eyed mystery woman. She was branded on his skin and still raging in his blood.

But who was she? And what had she been doing in that old cabin last night?

He'd been sent to that clearing, drugged, his horse shot and thrown from his mount to be injured. How had he ended up in the arms of a woman?

His every instinct told him that all of it—including the woman—was part of something much larger. But what? How could any of this tie in with his mother's murder thousands of miles across the sea in another country?

Even with his screaming headache, it was clear what he had to do.

Find the woman.

And get the truth out of her.

ON RETURNING TO THE RANCH, Rory stopped only long enough at the mailbox on the county road to pick up her mail.

Another official-looking letter from her royal neighbors. She cursed under her breath, then reminded herself cursing wasn't very ladylike and only proved that what Griff had said about her was true.

She cursed at the thought—and Griff—as she drove to the ranch house. She didn't bother to open the letter, knowing it was just another offer on her ranch from her new royal neighbors.

She tossed the offer into the fireplace. How many times did she have to say it? No amount of money could make her change her mind about selling her ranch.

They'd thrown serious amounts of money at her already, as if convinced she could be bought—the price just hadn't been agreed on yet. She'd written them numerous times and even called twice, both times being told she should leave a message since it was impossible for her to speak to Her Highness.

Maybe in the princess's country she could force Rory to sell, but they were in America now.

More to the point, they were in *Montana*. Montanans didn't take kindly to being pressured into anything, especially when it came to their livelihood.

In Montana people like her felt that not only did they have the right to protect their land, they were also capable of doing so. It was one reason there were more shotguns over the fireplaces in this state than in any other. There was still a little of the Old West alive and well up here, and her royal neighbors were going to find that out if they didn't leave her alone.

THE WOMAN WITH THE GREEN EYES haunted Devlin through-out the rest of the day as he worked in the stables with the other grooms. Several more guests had arrived.

But the guest who had the grooms gossiping when no nobles were around was Lady Monique Gray.

"They call her the Black Widow," one groom confided. "All her husbands die."

"Which makes her richer than the king," one said.

"Not the king," another argued. "But richer than us, that's for sure."

They all laughed.

"She just buried the last one, so you know what that means. She's here looking for her next prey."

"Maybe back to even the score with her former lover, Lord Alexis. I heard she threatened to kill him if she ever saw him again."

The servants of the court did love the drama that always surrounded royalty.

"I say the Black Widow has her eye on the Prince himself," interjected one groom.

The others exchanged nods.

"If that be the case, then I'd wager the king sent her so he could finally get Broderick out of the family," the groom said quietly, afraid of being overheard. It was one thing to speak of lords and ladies. Another to be heard disparaging the royal family.

Devlin only half listened to the gossip. He'd heard enough about Princess Evangeline that he doubted she would allow anyone to steal her husband.

He left the group to see if he could find Nicholas as he was returning from his ride.

"I'm sorry, Dev. I can't say who left the main parlor after you last night. I had to make a phone call before dinner. All I can tell you was that everyone was in the dining hall when I arrived for dinner."

"But someone could have followed me and gotten back in time to dress for dinner?" Devlin asked.

"I suppose they could have. You're that convinced it was one of the guests?"

"I'm just trying to consider all the possibilities." He thought about mentioning the green-eyed woman. She hadn't been one of the royal guests staying at Stanwood. If she was one of the servants, Nicholas wouldn't know. Maybe when Devlin had more information about her, he'd ask for Nicholas's help. But for the time being, he would keep the woman to himself.

It wasn't until later, his work done for the day, that Devlin saddled a horse on the pretext of exercising it. He planned to take a circuitous route to the cabin he'd awakened in that morning. Just in case he was being followed.

He couldn't wait to find a clue to the green-eyed woman haunting his every waking thought.

That was probably why he didn't notice someone standing in the shadows of the stables as he left.

Only one set of eyes seemed to follow his departure with interest. The dark blue eyes of Princess Evangeline.

RORY TOLD HERSELF she had no choice but to return to the line shack and retrieve her horse blanket. But this time, she felt even more nervous about trespassing—let alone getting caught.

What if the groom had told someone about her?

As she neared the line shack, Rory slowed her horse. A magpie cawed from a pine as she dismounted in the trees several dozen yards from the shack. The sky overhead was blue and cloudless after the storm last night, the peaks lightly dusted with fresh snow.

A slight breeze stirred the heavy boughs of the pines, emitting a soft sigh, as Rory walked toward the shack, her senses on alert. She half expected to hear the sound of hooves pounding in her direction. Light and dark played in the thick stand of aspens as she glanced in the direction of the royal palace, but she saw no spotted horses, no fancy dressed grooms, nothing but sunlight and shadow.

At the shack door she hesitated, listening for any sound within before she pushed it open. The hinges groaned loudly, the door giving only a few inches, the noise making her jump. She let out an embarrassed, nervous chuckle and started to enter when she heard a familiar sound that stopped her cold.

The jingle of a bridle. She'd know that sound anywhere. Leaving the door ajar, she hurriedly stepped to the side of the shack, flattening herself against the outer wall as she heard a horse snort. The snort was followed by the sound of horse's hooves in the fallen leaves of the aspen grove on the far side of the shack.

Rory glanced toward her own horse, only partially visible through the pines, and prayed the mare didn't make a sound. Fortunately her horse seemed more interested in munching the tall grass.

The creak of leather made her freeze as she heard the rider dismount. The horse let out a shudder and pawed at the ground, taking a few steps closer to where she was hidden.

The door of the shack groaned all the way open. Silence. Then the heavy tread of boots on the worn wooden shack floor as the rider entered the building.

Rory didn't dare breathe. What could someone be doing in there?

More footfalls on the wood floor. The line shack door groaned closed. She heard him swing up into the saddle, the leather creaking again, the sound of the horse moving, and feared for a moment he might ride in her direction and see her.

Silence.

She hadn't heard him leave. Was he just sitting there?

Unable to stand it a second longer, Rory edged to the corner of the shack and peered around it.

Her heart jumped.

It was the groom from last night.

A gasp caught in her throat.

He had her horse blanket in his hands and was studying the lettering in the leather.

She ducked back, cursing silently. To hell with the horse blanket. It was too late anyway.

With relief, she heard him ride away from her, back in the direction he'd come, back toward the royal kingdom he must still be employed by. So he hadn't gotten fired and sent back to his country.

Rory would have been relieved—if he hadn't taken her horse blanket.

Her pulse thrummed in her ears.

Was it possible he was looking for her?

Why else return to the line shack? Why else take her horse blanket with him?

He was trying to find her.

But why?

Chapter Six

It had come back to him, standing in the shack over the horse blanket. The images of the green-eyed woman in the throes of lovemaking had almost dropped Devlin to his knees.

He felt confused by the images, worse by the emotions the images evoked. The woman had touched him in a way that surprised and angered him. Clearly, she'd done her job well. But to what end, other than to lure him to the woods so she could seduce him?

He ground his teeth at the thought that he'd let himself be deceived in such a manner.

Well, the woman would answer for it when he found her. And he would find her—and her accomplice. Someone at Stanwood knew the truth and he was bound and determined to find them.

Devlin rode the horse a few yards into the trees, then circled back. He'd seen the fresh tracks around the old shack. His instincts told him that whoever had been there, hadn't left. He feared that after last night, he couldn't trust his instincts.

But he'd been right about the green-eyed woman. She *did* exist. All-around Best Cowgirl. Oh, yeah, she existed all right and he had a feeling he was about to find her.

He eased through the pines until he could see the back side of the shack. Just as he'd thought, a figure moved from the shadows along the side and headed into the trees.

He frowned. It didn't appear to be a woman. Western hat pulled low, large old worn jean jacket, jeans and boots. A horse whinnied in the distance. Whoever it was had ridden there.

Just as he'd feared, his horse let out an answering whinny. He spurred his mount as he heard the pounding of horse hooves as the person took off.

Devlin caught sight of the rider racing through the pines and went after him. He loved nothing better than the chase. The wind in his face. The powerful horse beneath him. The knowledge that no one could outrun him. Not on a horse. Especially the one he was riding.

But the rider in front of him was giving him a damned good run. Devlin pushed his horse, gaining on the horse in front of him. The pines parted in a wide open meadow rimmed in aspens. Devlin drew alongside, both horses running flat out, neck and neck.

That's when he saw not only that the rider was female— but very familiar. Fear flashed in a set of beautiful green eyes. The same beautiful green eyes that had been haunting him since last night.

Reaching over, he grabbed her reins, drawing both horses up. His horse danced to a stop under him as hers bucked.

Devlin bailed off his horse, grabbed her by the waist and swung her down to the ground, surprised how well she'd managed to stay on the bucking horse.

"What are you doing?" the woman demanded. "You could have gotten us both killed!"

Her hair had come loose of the Western hat. She jerked the hat off and slammed it on her pant leg. Chestnut curls tumbled around her shoulders. Devlin remembered the feel of her hair beneath his fingertips. Remembered those eyes firing with passion in a flash of lightning. Remembered the body hidden beneath the oversized worn jean jacket she now wore.

"It's you," he said, sounding as breathless as he felt. His gaze lit on her mouth and he was struck by the memory of the taste of her. For a moment, he forgot that this woman was part of a plot against him.

"Who hired you to lure me to that shack last night and seduce me?" he demanded, towering over her as that memory came back to him.

Those green eyes flashed with fury. "*Excuse* me? You're the one who seduced *me.*"

"That's not the way I remember it."

"I'm surprised you remember anything given the shape you were in," she snapped.

"I remember," he said, his gaze locking with hers. "I have flashes of you naked in my arms."

Her cheeks flamed, but she didn't break eye contact. "From that, you decided I was part of some kind of diabolical plot against you?"

He grinned. "I have to admit that part of the plot did make me wonder."

"If you remember as you say, then you'd know that I saved your life," she said with a shake of her head.

"You saved my life?" He let out a humorous laugh. "You were in on the plot to get me to that shack. Don't deny it. I found your horse blanket."

"I don't know what you're talking about, but I want my blanket back," she said reaching for it.

He stepped between her and his horse, where her horse blanket was still thrown over his saddle. They were so close he could feel her warm breath brush his cheek. "If you didn't lure me to the cabin, then how was it you just happened to be there?"

"Luck. *Good* luck for you. If I'd left you out in that storm after you got thrown from that beautiful horse you were riding, I doubt we'd be having this conversation right now. But then again, as drunk as you were, maybe the alcohol in your system would have kept you alive."

"I wasn't drunk. Someone drugged me."

She raised an eyebrow. *"Drugged?"*

He nodded, scowling at her. "And that beautiful horse I was riding? Someone shot it with a pellet gun to unseat me."

Her horrified expression surprised him because it appeared to be genuine. "Who would do such a thing?"

"Why don't *you* tell me?"

"If you think I would be involved in anything that injured a horse…" The ferocity of her words made him take a step back to study her.

"Okay," he said, finding himself at least wanting to believe her. The fall air smelled of pine and fallen aspen leaves. He breathed it in, picking up the fresh scent of the woman, as well. The last of the day's sunlight caught in her hair, turning it to spun gold.

"So you're trying to convince me that what happened wasn't planned?"

She snorted under her breath. "Not on *my* part."

The breeze rustled the aspens. A moment later, they were showered with dried leaves that danced around them like snowflakes.

He watched her shake off the leaves that caught in her hair.

"You never said what you were doing there last night, if not waiting for me." He couldn't help being suspicious.

"Actually, I suspected you were following me." She sighed

again and he could see her making up her mind whether to tell him something as she settled her hat back on her head. "I was checking out the royalty and got caught in the storm."

He wouldn't have taken her for one of those people impressed by royalty.

"I knew where the line shack was so I headed for it. When I heard your horse and looked out to see you on the ground, I braved the storm to bring you into the line shack, where you hogged my horse blanket. You were so drunk—"

"Drugged."

She sighed. "Fine. Drugged. You called me a forest sprite and asked how you would ever be able to repay me for my kindness. Right before you passed out."

Her words had such a ring of truth to them… He cringed at how he'd repaid her. "If you're telling the truth—"

"Of course I'm telling the truth."

"Then someone didn't expect you to be there and take me into the line shack."

She brushed her hair back from her face as another gust scattered leaves around them. "I did hear a horse nearby and thought you might not have been riding alone, but the other mount went back the way it had come."

So there had been someone out there. Maybe the plan *had* been to finish him off if being drugged and thrown from his horse didn't do the job.

As he looked at the woman, he realized she very well may have saved his life. *If* she was telling the truth.

He pulled her to him, his mouth dropping to hers. She tasted familiar. He felt desire shoot through him as their lips touched. He'd definitely made love to this woman. The experience was burned in his soul.

The kiss brought back the memory of her warm and willing

in his arms and left an ache when she pulled back to glare angrily at him.

But the kiss was impulsive and dangerous. What *had* he been thinking? That from one kiss he could tell whether she was lying or not....

"That might have worked once," she said, sounding as breathless as he felt. "But this time we're not sharing a horse blanket."

"I had to know the truth." The truth was he'd been dying to kiss her from the moment he'd pulled her down from her horse and seen it was the same woman from last night.

She cocked her head at him. "That was a *test?*" She seemed amused by that. "I guess I passed." She reached for her horse's reins. "I'd like my horse blanket now," she said, tilting her chin skyward.

"Not until you tell me your name."

She shook her head. "It's better you don't know." She swung up into the saddle.

"I can find out. All-around Best Cowgirl. Whitehorse Days."

She held out her hand for her blanket. "My name's Rory." She cocked an eyebrow at him.

"Devlin Barrow." He handed her the horse blanket. "You have a last name?"

They both turned at the sound of riders coming their way.

RORY SPURRED HER HORSE at the sight of the royal guards riding in their direction and took off, making a beeline for home. All she could think about was getting away from Devlin Barrow.

She was still shaken by her encounter with the groom. All her bravado when she'd been caught by him was long gone. He was even more handsome in the daylight. The kiss had brought back last night and the emotions he'd evoked in her, as well as the desire.

What he must think of her. Worse, what would he think once he knew who she really was? Not that brazen woman from the line shack, that was for sure.

Wouldn't he be surprised to find out she was the woman who refused to sell to his employer.

She glanced back, half afraid he and the royal army were following her. They weren't. She could see his broad back and the way he was standing to face them. If anything he was trying to protect her, she thought with a stab of guilt. She'd run out on him, leaving him to face the consequences.

But Rory assured herself that being caught with her wouldn't have helped his case.

She realized that she believed his story about being drugged and his poor horse shot with a pellet. Maybe there was something to his kiss test after all.

It felt odd, trusting a complete stranger. Except it hadn't felt like that between them. It was as if they had shared more than a night of passion. She'd been joking about saving his life. Kinda. But maybe she had.

Odd as it seemed, she felt as if she knew him.

She could just imagine what Georgia would have to say about that.

Rory just hoped he was all right. Surely those soldiers wouldn't do him harm. And yet even as she thought it, she realized that if she really did believe him, then someone had tried to do him harm just the night before.

She shuddered at the thought. Who would want to hurt a royal groom? Or was it possible that it had something to do with her and her ranch?

Maybe Griff was right. She was seeing conspiracy plots everywhere she looked. But so was her royal groom, then.

Suddenly, all thought of the royal groom or the deputy flew out of her head as she saw where her barbed wire fence had been cut. Not just in one spot but several.

Rory drew up her horse and swung down from the saddle. There were tracks in the soft earth. Boot tracks. Man-sized.

She cursed as she picked up one end of the barbed wire and inspected the clean cut.

Vandals? Or had someone been looking for fresh beef still on the hoof?

The problem was there weren't any cattle being run in this section, so why cut fence? No fool rustler would cut the fence without first seeing cattle on the other side.

Not only that—whoever had cut the fence had apparently walked in from the road—a good half mile away.

Rustlers tended to steal cattle close to the road so they could be quickly loaded into a trailer for a fast getaway. Also, most rustlers worked in pairs. Whoever this was had been alone from what she could tell of the tracks.

This hadn't been a rustler. Nor some drunked-up kid out to destroy property because his girlfriend had dumped him.

No, this person had to have had another reason to vandalize her property.

Rory glanced back the way she'd come. She could see part of the royal family's palatial roofline above the trees.

She shifted her gaze to the two spots where her fence had been cut. This felt more like a warning.

Whatever it was, she was going to have to call the sheriff's department again and that was something she really wasn't looking forward to.

PRINCESS EVANGELINE watched her husband come into their suite. He hadn't seen her, didn't realize she'd returned.

Broderick went straight to the bedroom. She could hear him in there opening and closing drawers.

Quietly, she got up from where she'd been sitting and moved to the bedroom doorway in time to see him emptying his pockets into one of the drawers. He caught his reflection in the mirror as he closed the drawer. All his attention went to his face.

Hurriedly he wiped at a spot on his cheek, then spun toward the doorway as if sensing her there. She saw the startled, guilty look in his eyes. It was easy to recognize since she'd seen it so many times before.

"Evangeline," he said on whiskey-scented breath. "I didn't realize you were here."

"So I gathered," she said stepping deeper into the room. The scent of whiskey did little to mask the underlying sweet odor of cheap perfume. She blinked back tears, surprised that Broderick could still disappoint her.

Had she really hoped that he would quit his philandering once they were in the States? Then that would make her a bigger fool than even her husband.

"I see you're up to your old tricks, so to speak," she said, furious with herself for thinking he might be capable of change. "You always did stoop to the lowest point possible."

"My dear, my dear," Broderick said with a laugh. "Are we to resort to name calling? I think you might want to reconsider. You know what they say about mudslinging. If you can't take wallowing in it yourself—"

"Aren't you afraid I'll grow tired of your antics and have my father terminate our marriage and throw you back into the gutter where I found you?"

He smiled. "So you admit you knew what I was when you married me. A gambler, a womanizer, a rogue. That, my dear, is what you fell in love with and that's what you get," he finished, throwing his arms wide with dramatic, drunken theatrics.

"You're drunk," she snapped.

"How else could I put up with your tedious lectures?"

She grabbed his arm as he started to turn away. "If I told my father, he'd have you killed."

Broderick laughed. "Not before I told him about you and Alexis and the others." He quirked an eyebrow. "What? You didn't think I knew? While you might be more discreet than I am, you are none the less innocent, my dear. Your exploits, like mine, are legendary. That's why we're made for each other."

"I know you're seeing someone."

"Seeing someone? What a quaint expression."

"You are supposed to be buying up land for my father," she said, growing angrier by the moment. She could just imagine the kind of woman he'd been with. It turned her stomach.

"Haven't I always done your father's and your bidding, my dear?"

"What about the Buchanan property? I assume you closed on it and were celebrating."

He scowled at her. "I'm working on it."

"So you haven't gotten anywhere with the owner."

"Rory Buchanan. Not yet."

"Have you even been over there to talk to the man?" Evangeline demanded.

"I'm taking care of it, trust me."

"I don't trust you and you've already wasted enough time." Evangeline had hoped that buying up land would keep her husband out of trouble. She should have known better.

A laugh floated up to the open window. Lady Monique Gray's flirting laugh.

"Is that who you've been with?" Evangeline demanded,

wondering where the devil Laurencia had been since she had been ordered to keep the two apart at all costs.

"Monique isn't here because of me."

Evangeline didn't believe him for a moment. She rang for Laurencia but got no answer. "Did you happen to see Laurencia on your way in?"

"Laurencia?" There was contempt in his tone. "Sorry, my dear, it appears another of your schemes isn't working so well," Broderick noted with no small amount of scorn.

She shot him a murderous look before pushing past him to storm out of the room.

To Devlin's relief, the royal soldiers were simply riding the property as per orders by the head of security, Jules Armitage.

The lead soldier had recognized Devlin as one of the grooms and apparently the group hadn't seen Rory. Devlin had stepped out of the trees to meet them, hoping to give her a chance to get away.

And she had gotten away.

Again.

But at least now he had a first name. And the information from her horse blanket. Her quick escape had him all the more curious about her. She didn't act like a woman who had nothing to hide.

As soon as everyone cleared out of the stables, Devlin used the phone to call the town of Whitehorse. The small Western town was just down the road.

It took several calls to find out who kept records of winners from the annual Whitehorse Days rodeo. He was directed to one Miss Adele Brown.

After four rings, an elderly woman finally picked up the phone. "Hello?" She sounded ninety if a day.

"Adele Brown?"

Silence, then a weak, "Yes?"

"I recently moved to the area and I'm interested in finding out about Whitehorse Rodeo Days. In particular, I'm trying to find out about your former All-around Best Cowgirl winners. I was hoping you could help me."

"I suppose so. I could tell you weren't from around here," she said with a chuckle. "If you tell me the year, I'm sure I can tell you who won All-around Best Cowgirl."

He breathed a sigh of relief. This had proved to be easier than he'd thought. "It would have been 1997. I have her first name. Rory."

"Oh." He could almost hear her purse her lips. "I was afraid of that."

"Excuse me?"

"You weren't around so you wouldn't know about our office burning down in 1999," Adele Brown said. "It was one heck of a fire. The fire marshal suspected it was arson, and land sake's, it was. The entire county was shocked when they heard who had started the fire. Misty Justin from up by Stinky Creek. Seems she was mad because she lost. Can you believe that?"

"So what you're saying is…" He'd jumped in at the first opening.

"Everything burned up. Records and all. I can probably give it some thought, ask around and come up with a name if I put my mind to it over the next few days. But the name Rory doesn't ring any bells at the moment. Must not be from White-horse, and right now I've got cinnamon rolls cooking in the oven that I have to see to."

Before he could tell her that he might not have a few days, Adele hung up.

Chapter Seven

As Rory rode up to her ranch house, she spotted a large dark car waiting for her out front. Was it possible the groom had already found her?

No, she was willing to bet it was about buying her ranch. She thought of her cut fence and reined in her horse, wishing she could rein in her temper as easily.

Sliding out of the saddle, she walked her horse slowly toward the waiting car and the confrontation she knew was coming.

As a man emerged from the backseat of the car she saw from the way he was dressed that he was from the royal family next door. The dark three-piece suit was a dead giveaway. Only undertakers and lawyers wore suits in this part of Montana.

"Is Rory Buchanan available?" the man asked in that now familiar foreign accent. "I would like to speak with him on a matter of shared importance."

She smiled, amused, although it wasn't the first time someone had thought Rory was a male name. "*I'm* Rory Buchanan."

The man's gaze widened only slightly. "I see."

She figured he did as she put her hands on her hips, knowing what was coming next.

"Prince Broderick Windham," he said with a slight bow.

"I have come in the name of Her Royal Highness Princess Evangeline Wycliffe Windham to make an offer on your property," he said, pulling out a long white envelope from his breast pocket beneath his coat. He held the envelope out, but she didn't move to take it.

"My ranch isn't for sale," Rory said calmly, not in the least impressed that the prince had come himself to make the offer. "I believe I've made that perfectly clear. So you can stop cutting my fence because it isn't going to make me change my mind. All it's going to do is make me madder."

The man frowned, looking confused. "I wouldn't know anything about your fence."

She almost believed him. "Right." She turned to lead her horse toward the corral.

"You might want to take a look at the offer," he said behind her.

She turned back to him. "I said no. And I mean *no*."

"We both know you'll sell eventually. It would be in your best interest to sell now," he said biting off each word.

Rory's gaze drilled the man. "That almost sounded like a threat." She caught the smell of alcohol and something sweet like perfume.

The prince sighed. "The Princess, the only daughter of King Roland Wycliffe, wants your property. We can save ourselves a lot of trouble if we settle this now. Just tell me how much you want." He pulled out a checkbook and pen and looked up at her expectantly.

Jamming her hands on her hips again, she stared at him in disbelief. "How many times am I going to have to say this? My land isn't for sale at *any* price."

"I don't think you understand—"

"Oh, I understand. But I'm not selling. Especially to your

princess. I don't like the way you do business. I don't like you buying up Montana. I wouldn't sell to you if I didn't have a dime and was starving to death. And tell your Royal Highness for me that if any more of my fence gets cut I'm not going to call the sheriff. I'm going to come over there personally."

The prince smiled as he knew what a waste of time that would be for her. He slowly put the pen and checkbook away. Clearly, he didn't see her as much of a threat.

"I'm sorry you feel that way," he said smoothly, "but I can assure you Her Royal Highness had nothing to do with the cutting of your fence. Perhaps someone has played a joke on you."

"Some joke. I think you'd better leave now."

He met her gaze. "I do hate to see you make a mistake you will regret."

Her eyes narrowed at the implied threat. The second within minutes. She thought about the shotgun just inside the back door of the house. Probably not a good idea.

"If you come here again," she said not mincing her words, "it will be *your* mistake. I'll call the sheriff on you." Like that would help. Since the sheriff was out of town. With her luck, Griff would come out again.

"Good day, then," the prince said as he turned and climbed back into his big black car with the dark tinted windows. The engine revved and the driver turned the car around.

Rory watched until it left her property and tried to calm down. It took all her self control not to get back on her horse and ride over to her neighbor's and demand to see the princess herself.

But Rory was certain someone would call the sheriff's department before she got near Her Royal Highness. And knowing Griff, she'd be the one to end up behind bars.

DEVLIN HAD the strangest feeling that someone was watching him as he hung up the stables phone after calling Adele Brown about Whitehorse Days. He'd unsaddled his horse as soon as he had returned to the stables. By now, he'd hoped to have the full name of the woman.

What he planned to do with it, he had no idea. After meeting her—and kissing her—did he still believe she had something to do with his being lured into the woods last night?

He knew he was in jeopardy the longer he stayed there. As Nicholas had said, clearly someone there knew who he was and why he'd come to Montana.

The stables seemed eerily quiet. It was late enough that no one was around. Or at least he'd thought that was true. Dust hung in the air along with the scent of horseflesh and oats.

He turned at a scurrying sound in time to see one of the house servants slipping past. Had she been eavesdropping on his conversation? Gossip was a pastime among the servants and grooms, he knew only too well. But if this information got back to the wrong person…

Devlin took off after her. The woman appeared headed for the grooms' cottages. Servants were forbidden to fraternize with the grooms and trainers, which would explain why she appeared to be sneaking along the side of the stables.

As she reached the end of the building, Devlin came around the corner, making her jump back in surprise at the sight of him.

She was much older than he'd first thought. As she raised her head, he saw her face. "Anna?" His mother's friend and housemaid.

She glanced around as if afraid of who might be lurking in the dark. "I shouldn't have come." She took a step back, her face a mask of terror.

Nicholas had sent her, just as he'd said he would.

"I must speak with you. No one will know," Devlin assured her as he took her arm and drew her into the shadows.

"I can't be seen with you," she whispered, sounding close to tears.

"You found my mother the night she was murdered," he said, keeping his voice low and watching the shadows for any sign they weren't alone. "I have heard that the person who killed her wore the colors of the crown. Is this so?"

She gave a quick, frightened nod. Tears welled in her eyes. "Your mother was kind and good."

"Yes," Devlin agreed. That's why her murder was such a mystery. Clare Barrow had worked with nobles all her life, teaching them and their children and grandchildren to ride horses, boarding their horses, training their horses, pampering both.

She wasn't the kind of woman who made enemies. Everyone loved her. She was beautiful in so many ways.

Devlin had always wished he'd been more like her instead of like the father he'd never known. His mother had raised him alone from birth. His father, Leonard Barrow, had been killed in an accident shortly after he'd married Clare. Leonard had never even known about his wife's pregnancy.

Devlin could only assume he'd gotten his impatience, his intolerance for most of the rich and privileged and his temper from his father. All these years he'd tried to be more like his mother, but he'd failed miserably.

Maybe that was one reason he refused to take the royal government's word that his mother had been killed by a stranger, a beggar who'd been passing through town even though Devlin's mother's stolen brooch had been found on the poor man.

If a beggar had come to the door, his mother would have offered him food and shelter. But not the brooch his father had given her on their wedding night.

Devlin suspected that the brooch had been put on the poor beggar so that Clare Barrow's murder would appear solved. Add to that Anna Pickering's disappearance shortly after she discovered the body—and the rumor that a man dressed in the colors of the crown had been seen running from the house.

"I have heard that she was still alive when you found her. Did she tell you who killed her? Is that why you're so frightened? Why you left and came to the States?"

Anna shook her head.

"But you must know something. Please help me. I have to know the truth." He saw compassion fill her lined face.

"The princess," she answered in a sob-choked whisper. "She has the papers. She knows your mother's secret."

"What papers?" His mother had never kept anything from him. Or had she?

"You are not safe here and if I am seen with you…" Anna pulled away to leave.

"Where are these papers?"

Anna hesitated. He could see that she wanted to help him but she was afraid for them both. "In the locked bottom drawer of her desk in her suite. But if you try to get them, you will be killed. Please, I must go."

Devlin felt her shudder just before she broke free of him to escape and head back toward the palace.

It was all he could do not to go after her. But he knew she was right. They must not be seen together. He had already jeopardized the woman's life by coming to Montana. If anyone had seen them talking…

Devlin leaned back against the wall of the stables, heart in his throat, and tried to make sense of what Anna had told him.

Princess Evangeline had papers that exposed some secret of his mother's? A secret that got his mother murdered?

Devlin glanced toward the palace and considered how he was going to get into a locked drawer in the princess's suite in a palace full of guards.

JULES ARMITAGE DROVE to the small western town of White-horse, Montana, to talk to Adele Brown that evening. For all the good it did. A fire had destroyed all the records?

"You didn't back up the results on a computer disk?" Jules demanded. He had thought his home country was backward. But then he'd never been to Montana before. "Someone else must have kept records."

Adele shook her head. "What would be the point?" She was a tiny gray-haired woman with sparkling blue eyes and dimples and the habit of smiling a lot. If her cheerfulness wasn't bad enough, the woman was completely disorganized. Her desk was covered in papers stacked so high, he could barely see her over the top.

"The point would be… Never mind." He had to bite his tongue since obviously the point would be that she would still have the records, she would be able to give him a name and he would be out of there.

"Funny, though," Adele said with a chuckle. "Wonder what it was about that year and that title."

He had to ask. "I beg your pardon?"

"You're the second person to ask about that particular winner," she said. "I can't remember the last time anyone asked. Around here, people only care about the year they or someone in their family won and they aren't likely to forget it, so…"

"I get the picture," Jules said irritably. "About this other person who was inquiring—"

"Like I told him, I'll remember who won that year. Sooner or later," Adele said optimistically.

"Did this other person give you his name?"

"Nope. I just assumed you knew each other since you both have the same accent."

Jules blinked. "Did the person leave a number for when you did remember?"

"Caller ID. I got it right here." She dug through the piles on her desk and came up with the number surprisingly fast, all things considered.

"Recognize it?" Adele asked as she copied it down for him on a scrap of paper.

"No, but apparently we're on the same mission." Jules waited until he got outside before he used his cell phone to dial the number she'd given him.

The line rang four times before a young male voice answered.

"Who is this?" Jules demanded.

Silence, then a timid, "Dunhaven."

Dunhaven? One of the grooms?

"Where have I reached?"

"Uh, the stables at Stanwood."

The stables. Jules clicked his cell phone shut and frowned. Devlin Barrow could have made the call. But why would he be searching for the owner of the horse blanket?

After what Jules had discovered in that horrible shack, wouldn't it seem likely that Devlin had known the woman in question?

RORY WAS mentally kicking herself for calling the sheriff's department. She'd already mended the darned fence and after her talk with Prince Broderick Windham, she had her doubts anything would dissuade the princess. So what was the point except to have the vandalism on record?

She dialed Georgia as she waited for a deputy to come out, wanting her friend to assure her she'd done the right thing.

"A man came into the shop a little while ago asking about you," Georgia told her. "He had a European accent and he wanted to know all about you and your family."

"You didn't tell him anything?"

"Of course not. But after he left he went across the street to Janis Ames's beauty shop and you know he got an earful. He knows you're out there alone."

Rory asked what the man looked like and the car he was in. "Prince Broderick Windham."

"He was a *prince?*" Georgia cried, sounding impressed.

"Georgia!"

"It's just that I've never seen a real live prince before. Especially one that good-looking."

Rory groaned. "Hello? The man is only a prince because he married the princess and he's trying to force me off my ranch. He made it clear that the princess gets whatever she wants."

"If it makes you feel any better, I heard around town that the princess's husband is a rake." Georgia read too many Regency novels. "His noble blood is very watered down. Anyway, they can't *make* you sell. Have you told the sheriff that the man threatened you?"

"Actually, the sheriff's out of town and one of the deputies is coming up the road now. I'll talk to you later."

The minute Deputy Griffin Crowley got out of the car and Rory saw who it was, she knew this had been a mistake.

"What's this about some cut barbed wire?" he demanded.

Rory gritted her teeth. "This morning I found where my

fence had been cut in two places and I just had a visit from a prince who threatened me if I don't sell."

Griff gave her a skeptical look. "Threatened what?"

"Said I was making a mistake I would regret and that the princess always gets what she wants." She saw at once that Griff wasn't going to take the threats seriously. She had to admit that they didn't sound as threatening when repeated.

"Yeah. Okay, let's go take a look at your cut fence," Griff said with little enthusiasm.

"I already fixed the fence. There were boot tracks, man-sized, in the dirt that led to that old mining road."

Griff had stopped and turned to look back at her, his gaze pinning her to the spot. "You already fixed the fence?"

"Yes, did you hear what I said about where the fence was cut? It's next to the princess's property."

The sheriff took off his Western hat and raked a hand through his hair before putting it back on his head again. "You aren't trying to tell me that this princess cut your barbed-wire fence."

"I doubt she did it herself," Rory snapped. "She has lots of people to do her dirty work. Georgia said the princess's husband, the prince, was in her shop asking about me and my ranch."

"There isn't any law against—"

"They're trying to run me off my ranch." Angry tears burned her eyes. She willed herself not to cry, but when she spoke, her voice broke. "You know this ranch has been in my family for more than a hundred years. I was born and raised here, my parents and sister are buried on the hill over there with the rest of my ancestors. This is my *home,* my *life.*" She swallowed, dangerously close to crying.

She would not be run off this ranch.

"You have any idea when the fence was cut?" he asked.

"The tracks looked fresh."

Griff kicked at a dirt clod with the toe of his boot as if avoiding her gaze.

"What?" she demanded. She and Griff went way back. And while it had been years since he'd put a frog down her shirt and rolled her in a snowdrift, she still knew him and knew this look.

He had the good grace to look uncomfortable. "Are you sure this isn't just a ruse, you know, a cry for help?"

"What?" He'd better not be saying what she thought he was saying.

"I mean is there any chance all this is just a ploy to get me to come out here?" He actually looked hopeful. "I did ask you to marry me and I thought maybe—"

"Stop!" She let out the breath she'd had trapped in her lungs, her blood pressure soaring. "If you're saying that you think I made up the story about the cut fence to get you out here—"

"I know how stubborn you are. If you changed your mind about my proposal, you might be embarrassed to tell me."

She really could not believe this. "Griff, I called the sheriff's department because someone cut my damned fence, snooped around my place and threatened me." She had to bite her tongue to keep from telling him she'd been hoping it would be any deputy but him who responded.

"Okay." He raised both hands as if in surrender. "I'll take another look around."

She knew how much good that would do. Turning on her boot heel, she stalked to the house, slamming the front door behind her for good measure, too furious to deal with Deputy Griffin Crowley right then.

Through the window, she watched him look around the yard half-heartedly until she couldn't stand it anymore and went back outside.

He didn't seem to hear her as she approached. He was moving along the side of the house, his head down. He suddenly stopped next to her bedroom window to bend down to pick up something.

As he started to pocket whatever it was, she demanded startling him, "What did you find?"

PRINCESS EVANGELINE had set her plan into motion and now she felt trepidation that this whole thing might blow up in her face.

She was taking a terrible risk. At worst, she could lose everything if her father found out what she'd been up to. At best, she could finally have the life she'd always dreamed of living.

As she stood at the window, surveying her domain, she realized, it wasn't enough. She'd built a replica of the palace back in her homeland, furnished it with the best that money could buy, indulged her every whim.

And still it wasn't enough.

Nothing seemed to satisfy this ache in her. Not food. Nor men. Nor possessions.

She told herself that once she gave birth to an heir to the throne, then she would have everything she wanted. Her father would finally see her value. And once Broderick was gone from her life, she could return home to take her place in society instead of being hidden away in this godforsaken place.

Scowling, she turned at the tentative knock on her door. "Come in," she said irritably, not surprised when Laurencia entered.

"I hope I'm not bothering you."

Sometimes Evangeline wanted to shake Laurencia until her teeth rattled in her head. The woman had no gumption, no backbone, no pride. What had ever made Evangeline think Broderick might be interested in the pathetic woman?

"Where have you been?" the princess asked impatiently. "Never mind." It was too late to do anything about Broderick and she wasn't in the mood for Laurencia's simpering.

"I just thought you'd like to know that Lady Monique sent me away, saying she needed to be alone, complaining of a headache."

Evangeline raised an eyebrow. So her husband hadn't been with Lady Monique after all. It must have been one of the servants. That would explain the cheap perfume.

"Prince Broderick left, saying he was going to buy that last piece of property as per your request."

Maybe Laurencia wasn't as big a fool as Evangeline thought. She was keeping an eye on both the prince and Lady Monique.

"It won't be easy to keep the two apart until the ball," Evangeline said more to herself than her companion.

"It might be easier than you think. I believe that Lord Alexis's being here has dampened the fires of her lady's desire for anyone else." Laurencia smiled.

Monique and Alexis. "I thought he had cast her off?"

"Possibly it was the other way around," Laurencia said with a sly smile. "There seems to be some embers still burning there."

Evangeline couldn't help but smile. Still, though, she knew her husband. And the Black Widow. "You shall continue to keep a close eye on Lady Monique."

"Of course," Laurencia replied with a small, amused curtsey. "And Prince Broderick as well."

DEPUTY GRIFFIN CROWLEY looked startled as he rose and turned around to face Rory. She'd seen him slip something into his pocket and now she saw his guilty expression and felt her heart take off at a gallop.

"What did you just find on the ground?" she demanded.

"Take it easy," Griff said as he slowly pulled a pair of wire cutters from his pocket.

Her pounding heart stuck in her throat. "You weren't going to tell me about finding those." It was an accusation, not a question.

"I was going to ask you if they were yours."

"You know they aren't mine. They belong to the person who cut my fence and now you've destroyed any chance of getting a clear fingerprint off them."

"This is why I wasn't going to show them to you," he said calmly. "In the first place, because of the type of handle on these there is little chance of getting a fingerprint from them. Also they're a common type of wire cutter sold at the local hardware store. Thirdly, even if they were the ones used to cut your fence, there is no proof of that. And what would be the point since you apparently already know who cut your fence."

Rory didn't like his tone anymore than she liked his attitude. "What were you going to do with them? Get rid of them so I wouldn't know you found them?"

"I didn't want to upset you anymore than you obviously are since they don't prove anything."

"Except that someone has been snooping around my house!" Flushed with anger, suddenly she felt herself turn to ice as she saw where he'd found the wire cutters. Right under her bedroom window. One of the limbs on the bushes had been snapped off where someone had stood next to the building.

Rory hugged herself as a shudder went through her. Her bedroom curtains were gapped open. Just enough that whoever had stood there could have looked through the window…

When had the person dropped the wire cutters? When had they been within yards of her house? Within yards of her?

Anger warred with the cold tentacles of fear that had wrapped around her heart.

"This is why I don't like you living out here alone," Griff said, pocketing the wire cutters again. "Rory, if you would just let me—"

"What I need from you, Griff," she said biting off each word, "is for you to stop my so-called royal neighbor from harassing me. Can you do that, Griff?" She was scared and crying and that made her all the more angry.

"Rory, for just once, can you stop being so strong and let someone take care of you?" He took a step toward her as if he meant to comfort her.

She stepped back. "I don't need anyone to take care of me." She wiped hastily at her tears.

"We all need someone, Rory."

"Not me." She swallowed and looked away, wishing it was true. The other night in the line shack had only made her more aware of the need deep inside her. Seeing Devlin again today, kissing him, had only made it worse.

She had missed the warmth of another person. Missed human touch. Missed the connection that went beyond mere sex. For that time in the shack during the storm, she'd been close to another person. And now she found herself aching for it again.

But those thoughts always involved dark blue eyes and a royal groom with a European accent.

Not Griff Crowley.

He stepped back, a pained look on his face.

She hadn't meant to hurt him. She pulled herself together. For weeks she'd told herself that if she could ride this out, her new royal neighbors would stop once they realized she really wasn't going to sell.

But that was before someone had taken an interest in more than her ranch. That was before Griff had found the wire cutters lying in the bushes under her bedroom window.

"You're a damned deputy sheriff. Can't you at least talk to the princess, warn her to leave me alone?"

"Rory—"

"You know who's doing this." Her voice broke. "If I'm right, this is just the beginning. When are you going to do something? When they burn down my house? Or worse?"

"Oh, for cryin' out loud, Rory," Griff snapped. "You're making too much of a couple snipped barbed wires. It was probably just kids messing around your place."

She stared at him, hearing the coldness in his voice, the anger.

"Maybe if you took all the offers on your place to the judge, he might think they constitute harassment. Without proof these people are threatening you, Rory, my hands are tied."

But hers weren't, she thought as she looked into the distance, where she could make out a portion of a royal roofline gleaming in the sun.

And it sure as the devil beat sitting around waiting for someone to save her since her life was visibly short of heroes.

DEVLIN WAS in the stables when Lord Nicholas Ashford found him.

"Let's take a ride," Nicholas suggested. "I need help on my cantering."

Devlin quickly saddled both horses, knowing that something must have happened and that was why Nicholas was providing them with an opportunity to be alone and talk.

It was dangerous, though. As head of security, Jules Armitage would find out. He was already suspicious of Devlin.

But nothing could have stopped Devlin from taking the ride with his friend. Whatever was wrong, Nicholas thought he needed to know about it—and at once.

They rode out across the wide pasture, the tall golden grasses swaying in the breeze in contrast to the fringe of deep dark pines in the distance. Overhead the sky arched from horizon to horizon, a blinding blue dotted with white cumulus clouds.

But it was the air that Devlin had come to appreciate in this strange country. So clear and crisp. He understood why Montana had been called God's country. It was as close to Eden as a man could get.

Unless, of course, the man was there for deceitful purposes and living in a viper's den.

"I saw Anna," Nicholas said as soon as they were out of earshot. "She told me she talked to you. The woman is petrified that she'll be found out. If she's caught, she'll break down. I thought I'd better warn you."

"I can understand her fear," Devlin said, drawing up his horse the moment they couldn't be seen from Stanwood. "I wish there was some way to get her out of Stanwood."

"Believe me, that would only draw attention to you," Nicholas said. "Someone already knows who you are and why you're here. Or at least suspects why you're here."

"Did Anna tell you what she told me?" Devlin asked.

Nicholas shot him a look. "Nobility such as myself? Not likely. She doesn't trust anyone. I'm surprised she came down to the stables. She wanted nothing to do with me. Which just shows she has good taste."

"I need to get into Stanwood proper."

"Of course. I could probably get you in for drinks again, if you're willing to get drugged again."

"Thanks, but I'll pass. No, what I need is the run of the second floor royal wing."

Nicholas looked at him as if he'd lost his mind. "Well, hell, I'll just ask Evangeline to give you your own key."

Aspen leaves rustled gently over their heads. "I have a plan."

"I was afraid you were going to say that."

"But I'll need your help."

His friend smiled. "You're determined to get us both killed, aren't you? So what do you need me to do?"

"It will be risky."

Nicholas laughed. "I would have been disappointed if it was otherwise."

"I need to get into Lady Evangeline's quarters."

Nicholas looked skeptical. "I can't even get you up on the second floor, let alone into the princess's quarters."

"Are there guards?"

"Two posted at the entrance to the royal wing. But even if there weren't guards, you'd be spotted immediately unless…"

"Unless I was wearing the same costume as someone who actually lived on the royal wing," Devlin suggested.

Nicholas smiled. "You *are* the same size as Broderick…"

"I'll just need a costume exactly like his."

His friend was nodding. "I think I can see to that since the princess has hired an in-house seamstress to make our costumes and asked for two of each in case anyone has a spill. There is nothing like royalty." He grinned.

"I assumed she would have the costumes made in-house so there was no chance of seeing anyone else in a costume like her own."

Nicholas nodded. "Ah, vanity. Anything else?"

"I might need a distraction to get upstairs."

"Now that is something I can definitely handle," he said with a laugh. "Leave it to me." He sobered. "You do realize that if you're caught up there…"

"Don't worry. I'll wing it."

"That is what worries me."

"GRIFF IS SUCH A JACKASS," Georgia cried when Rory called her and told her what he'd said about her alleged cut fence being nothing more than an excuse to see him.

"Tell me you didn't do anything that got you arrested," her friend said. "You aren't calling for bail, are you?"

"No, but it was all I could do not to deck him." Rory walked around the ranch house with the phone to her ear, still angry and frustrated. "I might have threatened to get my shotgun and shoot him."

Georgia groaned. "You told him who you suspected?"

Rory heard the misgiving in her friend's voice. "*I* know it sounds crazy. But who else has anything to gain by cutting my fence?"

"You can't think of anyone else you've ticked off lately?" Georgia asked only half joking. "Bryce isn't back in town, is he?"

Her former fiancé? She certainly hoped not. "You know I thought Griff couldn't shock me anymore after he asked me to marry him. But suggesting I cut my fence to give me an excuse to see him? Did I tell you he found a pair of wire cutters under my bedroom window?"

"Rory, that's frightening. That means whoever cut your fence—"

"Came up to my house, possibly looking in my window. Griff says it was probably just kids messing around."

"You're kidding? Well, I hope he plans to do something about it."

Rory sighed. "He says his hands are tied without evidence."

"What about the wire cutters?"

"Apparently they're a common variety that anyone could have purchased at the local hardware store."

"What about fingerprints?" Georgia asked.

Rory loved her for asking. They were both big fans of mystery novels and movies. "Griff says the handles wouldn't hold prints. He said he'd check, when I insisted. But as he pointed out, even if he found the prince's fingerprints on the wire cutters, it doesn't prove he cut my fence or that he was trying to force me to sell my ranch to him."

"But it would prove that he was on your property," Georgia said. "Oh, honey, I'm so sorry. Griff still doesn't think the answer is for you to marry him, does he?"

"He did. But, no, I think he's finally gotten the message," she said, remembering the ice she'd heard in his voice as well as the anger.

"So what are you going to do now?"

"I don't know." Rory feared the vandalism would escalate if she didn't sell to the prince and she wasn't about to call the sheriff's department again.

She would have to take care of it herself and said as much to her friend.

"Ah, I'm not sure that's a good idea, kiddo," Georgia said. "If you're right, messing with this bunch would be dangerous. Have you seen this princess who wants your property so badly?"

"Are you kidding? That place is an armed fortress."

"You aren't thinking about going over there again, are you? I mean after what happened the first time… Maybe you should come stay with me for a while," Georgia suggested.

"I will not be run off my own ranch."

"How did I know you were going to say that?" Georgia laughed. "Promise me you won't do anything…"

"Stupid?"

"I was going to say crazy."

"You know me so well."

"Actually… Have you checked your mail yet today?"

"Why?" Rory asked.

"I've heard some people are getting invitations to a masked ball at Stanwood on Saturday night," Georgia said.

"Believe me, I'm not invited."

"I guess not. But if you could get your hands on one of the invitations, maybe you could meet this princess and explain why you're not willing to sell your ranch. On second thought—"

"No, this is good. A masked ball? It's perfect. Meeting this princess wouldn't do any good, trust me. But Griff said if I had copies of all the offers, I might be able to prove harassment."

"Let me guess, you threw all of yours away?"

"If I could find copies, I could take them to Judge Randall…"

"Why do I not like the sound of this?" Georgia joked.

"Any ideas how I could get my hands on an invitation?" Rory asked.

She heard her friend hesitate. "If the royal couple had the invitations printed down at Harper's Print Shop here in town… Even with an invitation, you'll need a costume and I've heard that there are none to be had in the entire county at this late date, but I might be able to scare up something. As for finding your way around Stanwood, I would imagine the plans for the place are on file at Whitehorse Construction."

"The company where your sister Sara works?" Rory asked with a laugh. "I knew you'd help me," she said, feeling close to tears again. "I owe you."

She'd just have to make sure she didn't run into her groom, Devlin Barrow, on the grounds the night of the ball. Fortunately, a groom wouldn't be invited to the ball so she didn't have to worry once she got inside Stanwood.

Meanwhile, she thought, as she studied the darkening sky outside the window, she intended to lock her doors and keep the shotgun by the back door handy—just in case anyone came snooping around again.

Chapter Eight

The night of the Stanwood ball a huge harvest moon hung over the tops of the pines, spilling shimmering silver rays over the palace.

Millions of tiny lights glittered throughout the grounds. White carriages and the finest horses had been sent down to the parking area on the county road to collect the guests.

Princess Evangeline had sent out several hundred invitations to what she hoped would constitute Montana royalty.

"I want to share Stanwood with them for a night," she'd told Broderick when she'd announced she was hosting a masquerade ball.

He'd laughed pitifully at her. "You are so transparent, Evangeline. You know that few of them have ever seen a princess. You just want to show off."

She'd been instantly angered at his response. Probably because it was partly true. She knew rumors had been running wild about what a bitch she was because of the way she handled people during the building of Stanwood. She planned to squelch those rumors tonight. Everyone would see her at her best.

Broderick, meanwhile, would try to see Lady Monique

before the ball when everyone was busy—especially his wife. But Evangeline had foreseen this. Just as she had kept her husband busy since Monique's arrival.

For her plan to work, Broderick had to be desperate for his precious Black Widow. The drug Evangeline would put in his drink later would make this ball the success she was determined it would be.

As she watched her husband dress for the event she told herself that before this night was over, he would regret everything he'd ever said or done to her. She would make sure of that.

"This ball was the best idea I've ever had," she said.

Broderick lifted an eyebrow. "Or your worse mistake yet. Worse than coming to this godforsaken place."

"We are only here because you are a contemptible, lying bastard," she said glaring at him. She couldn't have hated him more than at that moment.

"That is why you and I are so perfectly matched," he said as he slid his mask into place, brushing a kiss across her cheek as he passed her on his way to the door.

"Before you leave, would you mind helping me with this zipper?" she asked as she reached for her costume. Not the one she would don later. That costume was hidden until the appropriate time.

"Where is your precious Laurencia?" Broderick asked, sounding annoyed. "I thought she saw to these matters."

"Lady Monique asked for her help dressing," Evangeline said, turning her back to her husband so he couldn't see her face. Or her his. She wasn't sure she could constrain herself if she saw the disappointment in her husband's face that Monique was otherwise involved.

"I thought that's why we had servants," he snapped. "It's bad enough you treat Lady Laurencia like your handmaid…"

"Since when do you care how I treat Laurencia?" she demanded as she waited for him to zip her.

"Evangeline," he said softly behind her, making her heart quiver. She hadn't heard him use that tone with her since before they'd married, back when he was trying to win her over. "When will you learn?"

He zipped the costume, his fingers brushing the tender flesh at the nape of her neck. She felt herself trembling. Worse, she felt herself weaken toward him, yearning for that tender tone, that tender touch.

"I need a drink," Broderick said, pulling away again as if he feared letting himself be drawn to her. He left, slamming the door behind him.

Evangeline brushed at her tears, straightened and thought of Broderick's funeral, the condolences and sympathy she would receive after the horrendous death of her beloved husband. That day couldn't come soon enough.

It would be all the more touching since she would be carrying the heir to the throne.

RORY BUCHANAN SHIVERED as she slid from her horse. She could see Stanwood through the pines and catch snatches of melody on the light breeze.

It took her only a few minutes to change into the costume Georgia had found for her—the last costume to be had in the county.

"It's not ideal, but it will hide your hair and, hey, how often do you get to wear a dress?" Georgia said, obviously seeing more humor in this than Rory.

"You don't really think I can ride a horse in that, do you?" Rory had exclaimed.

"So you ride over, change in the woods. Trust me, no

one will recognize you in this costume. That's what you wanted, right?"

Rory pulled on the black wig. She'd braided her chestnut locks so they would be easy to push up under the wig. Taking a deep breath, she straightened her dress and slipped on the mask. Now that she was there, she couldn't help being a little anxious.

She tied her horse, promising to return soon, and headed toward the back of the palace. She'd anticipated that there might be guards, but she didn't see any. To her relief she saw that costumed guests swarmed over an outside terrace. Music spilled out from the open French doors.

Rory studied the crowd milling on the terrace, half afraid she would see Devlin. But after the last time... She hated to think what the soldiers had wanted with him.

She wished she could forget him, but how could she forget the feel of his mouth on hers or the warmth of his body pressed to hers or the way he looked at her with those oh-so-blue eyes?

Her temperature rose a few degrees at just the memory. She fanned herself as she slipped up the stairs to the terrace and was instantly swallowed up in the crowd and the excitement in the air.

Rory moved cautiously toward the doors of Stanwood, expecting someone would stop her and demand to see her invitation. She'd hoped that by coming later as she had that she could go unnoticed.

As she slipped through the door, eyes wide at just the sight of the lavish costumes, decorations, furnishings, her heart pounded. As impossible as it seemed, the place appeared larger inside than it had even from the outside. She couldn't help but feel that she'd just stepped into a fairyland, where anything could happen.

The jewels alone were blinding, not to mention the extraordinary costumes. She felt like Cinderella *before* the ball in the understated costume and ballet slippers. She'd known better than to even consider high heels.

Griffin's description of her bit into her conscience as she watched women dressed in gorgeous costumes dance with handsomely attired men in a huge ballroom.

It made her think of being in the groom's arms, that feeling she'd had of being safe, being cared for, being a woman.

She swatted the thought away, annoyed with herself.

"Excuse me."

Rory froze at the sound of the voice beside her. Slowly she turned to find a waiter holding a silver tray filled with champagne glasses.

He thrust the tray toward her. "Champagne?"

She took one of the fragile stemmed glasses, concentrating on not spilling the bubbly liquid since her hands were trembling with nerves.

The stiff costume made her squirm beneath the starched fabric and the black wig was hot. She should have gone with her first instinct and come as Calamity Jane, the infamous woman outlaw.

But then, as Georgia had pointed out, everyone who knew her would have recognized her.

The ballroom was full, spilling over onto terraces from French doors that circled the massive room. She recognized people she knew drinking champagne and visiting with what had to be some of the royalty given the costumes and the weighty jewels that glittered under the crystal chandeliers.

Across the room, she spotted a wide staircase that wound up to the second floor. Near the top, she saw two guards standing at the entrance to a hallway that led to the south wing. Rory noted that the other hallway entrance had no guards.

She took a sip of the champagne, the bubbles tickling her nose, and she slipped deeper into the crowd as she debated how to get on that wing, which, according to the information Georgia had gotten for her, held not only the princess's suite, but some huge antique desk that had taken six men to carry up the stairs.

It was in that desk that Rory hoped she'd find what she was looking for.

DEVLIN BARROW moved along the edge of the ballroom that now swam in a sea of brightly colored masks and costumes. There was an air of anticipation mixed in with the orchestra music, the oceanlike roar of voices and the rattle of champagne glasses and silver trays as servants moved among the masses.

All of it turned Devlin's stomach as he watched the opulent extravagance in the name of royalty. He spotted Prince Broderick across the room, talking with Lady Monique and Lord Nicholas. None of the three looked in his direction but he saw Nicholas glance at his watch.

Devlin moved toward the bottom of the staircase and checked his own watch. Only three more minutes before—

He plowed into one of the guests, felt the slosh of icy champagne spill over his arm as he clutched the guest's arm to steady them both as they passed.

Devlin was only vaguely aware that the person he'd collided with was female. His fingers slid over the silken fabric of her sleeve as she slipped past him, both of them moving in opposite directions, neither apparently watching where they were going.

"Sorry," they both said at the same time. At the sound of her voice, his gaze leaped to hers and locked as she slid past, her head turning to look back at him.

Her green eyes wide with surprise.

Devlin felt as if he'd been jabbed with a cattle prod. He stumbled to a stop as the crowd filled in behind her. He would know those eyes anywhere.

In that instant, he'd seen something else in those green eyes. Not only had *he* known *her,* she had recognized him!

Rory! But what was she doing there? His heart began to pound at just the sight of her. It brought to mind the flickering light of the storm, those beautiful unusual green eyes and their lovemaking.

Not to mention the fact that now this woman was here and had recognized him. If he was wrong about her…

Devlin changed directions, fighting the swarm of partygoers, as he started after her. Rory was moving fast, winding her way through the crowd, heading for one of the terrace doors. Once she was through it and out in the night, she would be gone.

He couldn't let her get away. Not again.

HEART POUNDING, RORY BOUND through the open terrace doors, pausing to look back, afraid Devlin would come after her.

She told herself she'd overreacted. That couldn't have been the groom from the night of the storm. The man with the dark blue eyes she'd just collided with had been wearing the colors of royalty. Rory was certain no mere groom would have been invited to this ball.

But then she hadn't been invited either, and she was here. And there was no denying the way those blue eyes had looked at her. Had recognized her.

Her heart drummed, her skin rippling with memory of the man's touch, his voice.

"My fair forest sprite. You have bewitched me."

Words whispered into the hollow of her throat as his warm mouth moved over her skin.

She looked back and felt a shiver as she caught sight of him in the throng. Their gazes locked across the crowded room. His expression alone sent another shiver through her. There was both challenge and promise in his eyes. It left no doubt. He had recognized her.

And he was more than wondering what she was doing here.

She could have asked him the same question, given the way he was dressed.

He gave her a slight nod of his head, his eyes never leaving hers. She felt confusion and fear. What was he doing at the ball dressed as if he were royalty?

She couldn't move, couldn't breathe. Music, voices and laughter rode as one on the night air. Closer, there came a high-pitched *clink* as someone tapped a piece of silverware on one of the champagne glasses, trying to get the crowd's attention.

As the crowd all turned, Rory spotted Deputy Griffin Crowley. He wore his uniform and a thin black mask. He was looking around, frowning, almost as if he'd glimpsed her in the crowd.

Rory found her feet and fled.

DEVLIN HAD GONE AFTER HER but after a few steps had been impeded by the crowd. He saw that he would never be able to catch her without drawing attention to them both.

He swore under his breath, furious that he'd actually had her in his grasp, only to lose her again. He could only watch with frustration as Snow White disappeared through the French doors and into the night.

It took all his control not to say to hell with everything and chase after her.

A sound drew him back to the ballroom.

"May I have your attention please," Lord Nicholas Ashford called out over the crowd as he tapped a piece of fine silverware to his champagne crystal. "Your attention please."

The crowd began to quiet, heads turning to see why the music had stopped, why one of the royal guests was standing on the bandstand at the end of the great hall and addressing them.

Forcing away thoughts of the green-eyed woman, Devlin quickly turned toward the stairs at the opposite end of the great hall. He should have been closer, but he'd lost valuable time going after Rory as far as he had.

Now he might miss his chance to get on the royal wing, miss the chance to find the papers Anna had told him about that somehow involved the murder of his mother.

And yet the memory of those green eyes followed him like a sweet, seductive perfume. How he wanted to chase after her. The fact that she was here made him suspicious of her again. After the kiss he'd been so sure she'd been telling him the truth…

He forced her from his thoughts. Tonight was his only chance of getting upstairs. He had only a limited amount of time to get onto the royal wing, get into Evangeline's suite and find the papers.

He continued to move toward the stairs, weaving his way through the guests as everyone's eyes were on the bandstand and the handsome man before them. Someone handed Lord Ashford a microphone.

"If I may have your attention," he said into it. Expectation fell over the crowd as Devlin slipped to the bottom of the stairs.

"If Lady Gray would please join me," Nicholas said. There was a murmur of surprise, then a stirring as the Black Widow made her way to him.

Devlin caught sight of Lady Monique's intrigued expression as she joined Lord Ashford. Devlin started up the stairs, moving as if he knew where he was going, belonged there, had maybe forgotten something from his room.

"Lady Gray and I are going to sing a duet in honor of Princess Evangeline and Prince Broderick on this wonderful occasion," Nicholas announced as he took Monique's hand and smiled at her.

At the top of the stairs, Devlin glanced back. All eyes were on the two on stage as the orchestra struck up a tune and Nicholas moved closer to share his microphone with Lady Monique. Devlin could see Prince Broderick at the edge of the stage. The lord prince didn't look happy. Nor did he look as if he would be going anywhere until the two were off the stage.

Devlin walked with his head down as if his mind were on something else as he headed for the royal wing. Nicholas had given him directions to Lady Evangeline's suite and taken the dangerous risk of getting him a pass key from the laundry servant's quarters.

From out of the corner of his eye, Devlin saw both guards look in his direction. He muttered under his breath, staggered a little as if already drunk and walked past them without a look or a word.

His heart was pounding in his ears so loudly that he feared he wouldn't hear them if they called after him. He didn't dare look back.

At the door to the Princess's suite, he stopped. Out of the corner of his eye, he could see both guards at their stations down the hall. Neither was looking in this direction.

With shaking fingers he pulled out the key and opened the door to the suite and hurriedly stepped inside.

RORY WAS STILL SHAKEN after seeing the groom at the ball—dressed as a royal—and Griff. Unlike her, the deputy had probably been invited.

Devlin had seen her and started to come after her, but seemed to change his mind. She'd seen the anger and frustration in his expression. He'd wanted to chase after her but something had held him back. The same thing that had kept him from calling to a guard to stop her?

Which made her think that, as she'd suspected, he didn't belong at the ball anymore than she did.

Interesting, she thought as she circled around the palace and tried to decide what to do next. She stopped under some shrubbery, chastising herself for being so foolish as to come here tonight in the first place.

Getting into the ball had been easier than she'd hoped. So had mingling among the many guests. But getting upstairs to this massive desk was a much bigger problem than she'd thought it would be. She'd seen herself having a run of the palace simply because she was in costume.

Discouraged, she glanced upward. According to the plans Georgia had gotten her, the princess's suite should be directly—

Rory started at the sight of a strange light flickering in what was one of the rooms in the royal suite.

She moved to get a better look. The drapes were drawn, but through a space between them, she could see movement. It appeared someone dressed identically to her groom was in the room above her just beyond the parted curtains.

What was he doing in the princess's rooms? Or was that Prince Broderick dressed in the same costume? But if it was the prince, why was the man sneaking around with a small flashlight?

It had to be her groom. But what was Devlin doing in the

same room Rory herself had hoped to get into? Apparently they had more in common than she'd first thought.

She watched him. He seemed to be looking for something.

Her gaze took in a second set of French doors that led to the wide balcony, the drapes on its doors drawn. She let her gaze fall from the balcony down the lattice trellis to a small stone wall a few yards in front of her.

As a tomboy, she'd climbed her share of trees. It had been awhile, but she hoped now that it was a lot like riding a bike.

Cursing her costume under her breath, she considered taking the time to go back to her horse and change clothes since she had no reason to return to the ball—especially after seeing Griff in there.

Deciding it would take too long, she crossed to the stone wall, hiked up her dress and swung up to grab hold of the trellis, praying it would hold her weight as she began to climb.

DEVLIN COULDN'T HAVE missed the desk—even in the dark. It was huge and took up most of the room just off the balcony.

Using the penlight, he moved to it, noticing a second set of French doors that he assumed also exited to the balcony.

He knew he had to move fast. He was counting on both the prince and princess to remain downstairs at least until Nicholas and Monique finished their songs since Nicholas planned to make the most of it.

The bottom drawer was locked—just as Anna had told him it would be. Taking out the small tool he'd brought, he carefully pried the lock until it broke. Quietly, he opened the drawer.

He had no idea what these so-called papers looked like, not to mention the underlying fear that Anna might have been mistaken. Or that the princess had moved them.

Devlin tried not to think about any of that as he hurriedly

went through the drawer. He worried about making too much noise even though the guards were stationed at the other end of the hall and the noise from the party should mask any sounds he made.

Still, he felt exposed being in the princess's quarters. He might be in America, but he was a foreigner. If caught, he would be sent back to his home country. His punishment could be worse than death if he was seen as a traitor, or worse, a terrorist.

He knew that Princess Evangeline could be excessively cruel and, as the only child of the king, was given anything she wanted. She'd want his head if she caught him breaking into what was obviously an antique.

The manila envelope was at the very bottom of the drawer, tucked under some writing stationery. As he pulled it out he saw the government stamp. There was no address. His fingers trembled as he flipped the flap and pulled out the sheets inside.

The papers crinkled in his tense fingers as he saw the royal crest on the familiar document—and his name.

His birth certificate? Why would Princess Evangeline have his birth certificate?

His hands began to shake and he had to put the paper down on the desk to read it, fighting to focus the slight beam of the penlight on the words.

Confusion made the words blur. He'd come up here expecting to find something about his mother's murder.

As the words on the document came into focus, he felt his pulse jump. *What?* That wasn't right. He dropped the penlight.

His heart drummed in his ears and he felt his blood rush from his head. He slumped into the chair, as he snatched up the penlight to read the document again. It had to be a lie. These documents had to have been forged. But why?

Otherwise… Otherwise, he realized with a shock he held the reason for his mother's death in his hands.

His mother. If this was true, then she had lied to him. His father hadn't died before Devlin was born. His father was *alive*.

He heard a sound behind him and instinctively turned off the penlight. The chair under him creaked as he turned his head to look toward the French doors from the balcony, half expecting to find a royal guard with a weapon coming through them.

For the first time, he saw that the thick dark drapes weren't closed all the way. Through the narrow strip between them, he could make out the balcony and past that the twinkling lights of the grounds in the distance.

Nothing moved. For a moment he thought he'd only imagined the sound as he quietly tucked the documents back into the envelope as he rose from the chair.

The second set of French doors slowly opened, the breeze catching the drapes and billowing them out into the dark room.

Chapter Nine

A gust of cold night air stirred the papers on the desk. Even if he could reach the French doors behind him, Devlin knew he wouldn't be able to get out them without being caught. Hurriedly he stuffed the manila envelope beneath his costume jacket.

With no time to spare, he leaped behind the long thick velvet drapes as someone entered the room. He heard the doors close, felt the night breeze still.

Devlin held his breath, afraid to move a muscle for fear he would be discovered. He heard someone move to the desk, brush some of the papers on the edge. A moment later, a drawer opened, then another. Whoever it was seemed to be searching for something. His birth certificate?

He took a shallow breath, still shaken and confused by what he'd found as he listened to the intruder searching the drawers much as he had done.

He wished he had a weapon. He'd become an expert marksman thanks to Nicholas, who'd taught him to shoot. He could also fence. Neither helped at the moment, though.

Carefully, he inched to an opening between the drapes as his curiosity got the better of him. Who was searching the desk—and why? He feared what they would do when they didn't find the documents he'd taken.

In the glow of the lamp light, he saw the figure bent over one of the drawers, her black wig askew, her Snow White costume torn at the hem and a piece of what appeared to be a twig caught in the fabric.

Rory? What was *she* searching for? He willed himself to stay hidden until she found whatever she was searching for. Unless she couldn't find it because he'd already taken it.

THE ROOM WAS EERILY QUIET, putting Rory's nerves on edge. Unfortunately, it appeared that her groom had left before she got there. She'd been forced to turn on the desk lamp since she hadn't had the foresight to bring along a flash-light as he had.

What had he been looking for? The same thing she was? But why would he care about offers made on her ranch? Clearly, he wasn't royalty as his costume suggested or why did he need to be sneaking around the princess's suite?

Heart sinking, Rory realized she had no idea what kind of man Devlin Barrow was. Just as he had no idea what kind of woman she was, she thought as she finally found what she was looking for in the last drawer she searched.

The file was marked Buchanan Ranch.

Hurriedly, she pulled it out and leafed through the contents under the glow of the lamp light. Someone had written nota-tions on each copy of the offer that had been sent to her. She tried to read them, but she was too nervous. Especially since she thought she'd just heard a sound out in the hallway.

Just take the file and run!

She realized she should have brought something to carry the contents in. The file was too thick. There was no chance she could hide it under her costume and she had that climb back down—

She jumped at a key snick in the hall door lock.

Rory froze as she watched the doorknob turn, the door begin to open.

A scream caught in her throat as she was grabbed from behind forcing her to drop the file. A hand clamped over her mouth as a strong arm circled her waist tightly and she was dragged back through the dark velvet drapery to slam against the rock-hard body of a man who whispered, "Make a sound and we're both dead."

DEVLIN HELD THE WOMAN tightly in his grasp as the door from the hallway opened. Light spilled across the floor and under the thin space between the floor and the hem of the drapes.

The door closed.

He could see part of the room through the crack in the drapes and feared that he and Rory could be seen as well.

But he didn't dare move to the side for fear that the person who'd entered would hear him.

He caught a glimpse of the princess as she headed to the bed and bathroom area of the suite. Fear made him freeze at just the sight of Evangeline. If the two of them were caught here now…

He breathed a little easier as he heard Evangeline moving around in the adjacent room. This had been one hell of night, all things considered. Not only had he found out that his mother had lied to him his entire life, he'd discovered that his father was alive. And now here he was with this woman; their paths just seemed to continue to cross.

Now why was that?

He hoped to hell the woman wasn't a cat burglar. Or worse.

Devlin could feel Rory getting restless and knew she was thinking the same thing he was—that maybe this was their chance to get out of there before the princess came out.

But before he could make a decision, Princess Evangeline appeared again, only this time in a different costume.

It took him a moment to place the new costume. Wasn't it exactly like the one Lady Monique Gray had been wearing when she'd climbed up on the stage next to Nicholas? Odd that the princess would change into a costume like that of the Black Widow.

Royalty. He didn't even want to speculate as the princess left again.

Breathing a sigh of relief, he waited a few moments before he loosened his grip on the woman in his arms.

"Wait," he whispered next to her ear. He caught the clean scent of her and was transported back to that damned shack where they'd first met. He wished he didn't know this woman—know her intimately. Being this close to her made him feel things he didn't want to feel. Especially now.

What he'd found in Evangeline's desk drawer made him feel as vulnerable as the information made him. This woman, on top of that, knocked him off kilter.

He was more than confused. He was running scared and that made him all the more anxious to get Rory away from there so he could find out who the hell she really was and how she fit in to all this.

The problem was, how the devil were they going to get out of there *together?* Because there was no way he was letting this woman get away again.

PRINCESS EVANGELINE took the back way to Stanwood's guest wing. In one hand, she gripped the master key that would open

Lady Monique Gray's suite. In the other she carried the bag she'd retrieved from the pantry.

Her heart was pounding hard, expectation making her limbs weak. Everything had to be just perfect for this to work. If Broderick suspected for a moment…

She pushed the negative thoughts away as she stopped partway down the hall, looked around and, seeing no one, slipped the master key into the lock of Monique's room and stepped in, feeling like a thief in her own home.

Evangeline stood for a moment, hit with the scent of Monique's perfume. The smell made her nauseous. She tried not to think about her husband and Monique together or recall other times she'd caught this particular scent on her husband.

The silence assured her that Laurencia had been successful in detaining Lady Monique. Evangeline flipped the light switch and blinked at the cluttered suite. Clothes were strewn everywhere. If the woman was planning to seduce the prince tonight, her seduction clearly didn't include a romantic atmosphere.

After quickly cleaning up the room, lighting the candles she'd brought, setting out the drugged bottle of bourbon—Broderick's favorite—and putting the note next to it in a Monique-like scrawl, Evangeline waited.

She was suddenly very calm as she looked around the dim room. She'd seen to everything, including unplugging the lamps, leaving the area around the bed purposely dark.

She was ready. Slowly, she began to take off the costume a piece at a time, dropping each to leave a trail to the bedroom that any fool could follow.

Even Broderick.

By the time she reached the bed, she was naked.

Except for the mask.

RORY COULDN'T HAVE made a sound or taken a breath if she'd wanted to. Even if she hadn't recognized the man's voice, there was no mistaking the scent of him or the solid feel of his body. The sound of footfalls had long ago died off, and yet Devlin still held her tightly against him.

His breath tickled her ear. His body, so close she could feel way too much of him. She shivered and he drew her even tighter against him as if to keep her warm. The gesture touched her. Until she reminded herself that the man was holding her captive behind the drapes of the princess's quarters—and like her, he apparently had no business here.

So what *was* he doing here? Robbing the place? The thought turned her blood to sludge. If caught, the princess would think they were both burglars, Rory thought indignantly. Not that she hadn't planned to take the contents of her file. But it was a file on *her*...

"We have to get out of here," her groom whispered finally.

She couldn't have agreed more. She just wondered where he thought they were going.

DEVLIN WAITED until he believed the coast to be clear before he moved aside the heavy drape and drew the woman out the French doors to the balcony.

The balcony was large with huge planters. He pulled her into a shadowed dark corner. From here all he could see was darkness and pine trees. Nor did he think she could be heard should she decide to start screaming.

Grabbing her arm, he spun her around to face him. "What are *you* doing here?" he whispered hoarsely.

"What are *you* doing here?"

He tightened his grip on her arm. "You first."

"I'm here because your boss is trying to force me to sell my ranch. I'd thrown the offers away. I needed copies but because of you, I had to leave them in there."

"Wouldn't it have been easier just to ask for copies?"

"You really think the princess would have given them to me?" she demanded, pulling away.

She had a point. But breaking into the princess's suite… Was the woman crazy? No crazier than he was, he realized.

Just being this close to her and not being able to touch her was pure torture. The memory of their night together haunted him. He would gladly have thrown caution to the wind and taken her in his arms again had she let him.

But there was little chance of that as she leaned against the balcony railing, glaring at him. "Your turn," she said, her hands going to her slim hips. She looked adorable as Snow White. And a little ridiculous, under the circumstances.

"If I told you, I'd have to kill you," he joked.

"Funny."

"You have no idea."

She started to step past him.

"Where do you think you're going?"

"Back inside. I have to get those copies. I'm not leaving here without them."

"You go back in there and you're risking more than your neck. You're risking *mine*."

She slipped past him so quickly Devlin didn't catch her until they were inside the suite door.

Two loud pops reverberated through the room.

"What was that?" Rory whispered.

Devlin shook his head. "Either someone is opening champagne out in the hall," he whispered, "or there were gunshots in the room next door. Either way, we're out of here."

This time she didn't argue as they hightailed it out of the suite and back to their spot on the balcony. The moon had risen higher in the night sky, filling even the shadows of the balcony, exposing their hiding place.

Devlin saw something move below them in the darkness. A man watching them. He grabbed Rory and pulled her into a kiss, turning her so the man below them could only see someone dressed in the same costume as Prince Broderick kissing some strange woman. Nothing new there.

At first Rory struggled against the kiss, but after a moment gave into it, her arms coming up to circle around his neck. He loosened his grip on her as she deepened the kiss.

His mistake. She slipped from his arms and dropped over the side of the balcony railing. All he got was a handful of fake hair as the black wig came off in his hand.

Devlin lurched to the edge of the balcony, fearful that she'd fallen to her death. In the darkness, he caught sight of his green-eyed forest sprite clambering down the trellis.

His first instinct was to leap over the edge after her, but she was almost to the ground and heading for the trees. He thought about her damned copies, which she'd risked her neck for.

"Damned woman," he muttered under his breath.

But as he started to turn to go back into the suite, he remembered the man he'd seen watching them along the edge of the building. The man was looking after Rory.

The figure bled back into the shadows and a moment later rounded the edge of the building, heading back as if toward the ball.

With relief, Devlin saw that it was a sheriff's deputy, dressed in uniform and wearing a thin black mask.

Devlin waited until the deputy disappeared back inside. He could hear music and laughter floating up from the ballroom. Devlin had to finish what he started and yet he couldn't help but worry about Rory as he rushed back inside the suite and turned on his penlight.

The Buchanan Ranch file was on top of the desk. He scooped it up, stuffing it along with his own papers under his costume jacket.

Now how the hell was he going to get out of there?

FROM THE DARKNESS another man watched the deputy go back into the ball as what appeared to be Prince Broderick slipped back into the royal suite from the balcony.

It wasn't the first time Jules Armitage had seen the two in the same vicinity.

As he saw a strange light come on in the princess's suite, Jules debated what to do. Prince Broderick had left the ballroom earlier—not long after the princess. As far as Jules knew, neither had returned.

So if that was Prince Broderick in the royal suite, then why was he using a small flashlight?

Just as Jules's curiosity was peaked and he started to step from the shadows to alert the guards to check the suite, the light went out. The French doors opened and the man slipped out, closing the doors behind him.

To Jules's amazement, the man came to the edge of the railing, looked down for a moment, then swung over the rail and began to climb down the lattice.

The head of security reached for his weapon as the man reached the ground. He'd lost his mask on the climb down. As he turned, Jules saw that it wasn't Prince Broderick.

It was Devlin Barrow.

Jules stayed in the dark shadows as the groom passed by him. Finally, he would have the royal groom right where he wanted him.

Chapter Ten

Evangeline heard the snick of a key in the lock. Her heart was pounding, each breath a labor. So much was riding on her being able to pull this off tonight.

The door swung open on a soft *whoosh*. She waited, lay on the big bed, only dim candlelight flickering around her. She'd made sure he wouldn't be able to turn on a lamp. Around her, Monique's perfume scented the air, making Evangeline nauseous.

She could do this. She had no choice.

She heard the door close softly. She held her breath. If it was Broderick, he would do as the note in the hallway had instructed. When it came to other women, Broderick was accommodating.

The soft clink of crystal assured her he was now having the drink she'd left for him. The pills would take only a matter of minutes to work.

If he did as instructed… She heard the sound of him shedding his costume, and she tried to relax. He was following her orders. Only because he thought they'd come from Monique.

Evangeline tamped down her anger. She could be angry later. If the pills worked their wonder, he would be so out of it by the time he reached the bedroom, he wouldn't know she wasn't Monique until it was too late—if ever.

From behind her mask, Evangeline watched the doorway. She'd never had any interest in sex. Just as she'd never liked alcohol except for an occasional glass of wine.

For her, losing control was her greatest fear. Sex with the right man, she'd heard, could make a woman lose all control. The thought of a man having that kind of power over her terrified her—although she'd had nothing to fear with Broderick.

While Broderick's good looks had appealed to her for propagation reasons, his suave man-about-town charm had always left her cold.

But tonight she must be Monique, a tramp in heat. It would be her best acting role yet.

The doorway filled with the dark shadow of a naked man, relieving her mind that her plan was working as he stumbled and had to lean against the door jamb.

His face, like the room, was in shadow but she could imagine his smile, anticipation and excitement in his eyes. She would have liked to have seen it since she'd never had that opportunity as his wife.

Broderick had never even pretended to be madly in love with her. They both had known why he'd married her. She just hadn't realized he had never meant to impregnate her with an heir.

But after tonight, if the Fates were with her…

He staggered toward the bed, the drug giving him the appearance of being drunk. With luck he wouldn't remember anything.

As he neared the bed, she couldn't see *him* anymore than he could see *her* clearly in the near darkness—just as she'd planned it. Now, if he just followed the rest of her directions and didn't speak.

He chuckled, though, as he slipped into bed wearing nothing but his mask.

RORY HAD LOOKED BACK only once, afraid Devlin was in hot pursuit. Nothing moved in the darkness. Stanwood cast a long black shadow over the landscape. Along the edge of the building, she spotted a figure.

Not Devlin. But someone else. And she had the distinct impression the person was watching her.

She ran deeper into the woods, disoriented in the darkness and the dense pine forest. Her chest ached from running and she couldn't wait to get out of her ridiculous costume. As she stopped and caught her breath, she heard movement nearby. The soft rustle of dried pine needles, the blow of her horse as the mare snuffled some grass.

With relief, she moved toward the welcoming sound, anxious to end this horrible night. It hadn't all been horrible, she had to admit, remembering being behind the curtain with Devlin and kissing him.

But she hadn't gotten the copies of the offers she'd gone to all this trouble to get. And Devlin had proved to be less than a hero. She had no idea what he'd been doing breaking into the princess's desk. Not only that, he seemed to think she was again part of some conspiracy against him.

Men. No wonder she'd never found her Prince Charming.

Through the trees, she spotted her horse and rushed to the mare, grabbing the reins and swinging up into the saddle. From the time she was young, she'd preferred to be in the saddle more than anywhere else. Not much about that had changed. She felt safe, finally in her comfort zone, as she reined the mare around and headed for home, praying she wouldn't run into any of the royal guards.

Rory thought that once she left the princess's property, she would put this night and Devlin Barrow behind her. But even when she reached home, had stabled the mare for the night and gone inside, locking the doors behind her, all Rory could think about was the groom.

He was probably a thief. Or worse.

And yet she couldn't believe that a man who could kiss with genuine conviction—could be a criminal.

As much as she hated it, Rory found herself charmed by her mysterious groom as she shed her Snow White costume.

DEVLIN HAD PRAYED the trellis would hold his weight. It had. He knew he wasn't thinking clearly as he headed for his cottage to change. After that, he planned to go to the stables, saddle a horse and take the copies to Rory. Something told him there was a lot more to this woman.

It concerned him that the deputy had been watching them from the shadows. Devlin could only assume the law officer had been part of ball security. He couldn't have known whom he was watching. At least Devlin hoped not. Otherwise, wouldn't the deputy have stopped Rory as she'd left? And called the guard to arrest Devlin?

Devlin felt fear snake up his spine at the thought that Rory might have been seen with him. After what Devlin had learned tonight, that information could put her in danger. It was why he had to sneak over to her ranch tonight, drop off the papers and then keep his distance until he had this mess sorted out.

His mother had been murdered. Devlin had every reason to believe he would be next—especially when Princess Evangeline found her antique desk broken into and the documents gone.

At his cottage, he changed quickly into riding clothes. From the Buchanan Ranch file, he found the location of her ranch. No surprise, her property wasn't far from the line shack where they'd met. With the full moon, he should be able to find her.

He opened the manila folder and took out what appeared to be copies and the original documents. He knew a place he could hide the copies in the stables where they wouldn't be discovered.

The originals he would take with him. He had to get them off the Stanwood estate. It was his insurance policy—if he lived long enough to use it.

Just the thought that he was the reason his mother had been murdered filled him with fury.

At a soft tap at the door, he jumped. *Rory?* Crazy as it was, he hoped to find her when he opened the door. The woman hadn't just stolen his dreams. She'd captured his every waking thought as well as his desires.

He tried to hide his disappointment as he saw that the person huddled on his doorstep looking terrified wasn't Rory. "Anna?"

He quickly ushered her into his cottage, checking to see if she'd been followed. He saw no one in the darkness, but he knew that didn't necessarily mean anything.

"What's wrong?" he asked, seeing that she'd been crying and was now wringing her hands. She'd aged in the months since his mother's death, and he knew how it weighed on her.

"The guards are looking for me," Anna whispered. "I saw them waiting by my door and came right here."

"Guards? Why—"

She clutched his forearm. "I saw who killed your mother. I thought if I kept quiet…" She began to cry softly. "He came to your mother's house himself, dressed as a royal guard, but I recognized him. It was Prince Broderick. He took the papers and killed your mother. I thought he didn't know I was there, that I saw. I knew no one would believe me."

"I believe you." Prince Broderick had killed his mother. But on whose orders? "You can't stay on the grounds."

But where could he take her where she would be safe? He didn't know Montana and had little resources. But there was one person. His heart told him he could trust Rory. So had her kisses.

"You will come with me. I know a place you will be safe," he told Anna. "Stay here. I will return with horses. You must trust me." For his mother's memory, he couldn't let anything happen to Anna.

WHEN THE DEED WAS OVER, Evangeline freed herself of the weight of Broderick's body, shoving him aside to climb out of the bed.

She sat for a moment on the side of the bed, praying she now carried the heir she so desperately needed. The timing had been perfect, just as she'd planned it.

Now all she could do was wait. She rose, feeling exhausted, disgusted and furious with Broderick.

For a moment she considered taking the lamp base beside the table and crushing his skull with it.

Instead, she quickly dressed in the extra clothing she'd brought herself, stuffing the Monique costume under the bed for the maid to dispense with in the morning.

As she started out of the room, she made the mistake of looking back at Broderick passed out on the bed, the sheet thrown over his head, where she'd tossed it.

She took a couple of steps toward the bed, afraid of what she would do if she didn't leave at once. If she didn't get out of there now…

Quickly, she turned and headed for the door, surprised how late it was. The last thing she wanted to do was get caught by Monique. This had been humiliating enough as it was.

But as she neared the door, she saw something that made her stagger to stop. The floor was littered with each piece of his costume. Evangeline stared down at it, her blood thundering in her ears.

Nooooooo.

She spun and stumbled back to the bedroom doorway, all her fears hitting her in a rush. This couldn't be happening.

She charged the bed, jerking back the sheet. Too dark. Dropping to the floor, she found the cord for the lamp beside the bed. The lamp flashed on, blinding her.

Getting to her feet, she finally looked at the man lying passed out on the soiled sheets.

She had to cover her mouth to keep from screaming. The man on the bed wasn't Broderick. The man she'd just possibly conceived an heir with was Lord Charles Langston, the family attorney.

Had she been the kind of woman to faint, Evangeline would have. She stumbled back under the weight of what she'd just done, trying to make sense of what had happened. How could her plan have gone so awry?

Where the hell was Broderick?

RORY WAS DRESSED FOR BED even though she knew she wouldn't be able to sleep, when she heard the sound of horses approaching. She jumped up and pulled on her robe and, taking the shotgun from by the back door, moved swiftly through the dark house. Since finding out about the Peeping Tom at her bedroom window, she'd taken to locking her doors and keeping the shotgun loaded and ready.

Moonlight bathed the yard in silver. From out of the pines, two horses emerged. She recognized the horses first. The beautiful Knabstrups. She expected to see two royal soldiers astride the horses and shifted the shotgun, ready to defend herself and her property.

To her shock, Devlin Barrow swung down from the first horse, then went to help the other rider down. An older woman. He led her toward the darkened house cautiously.

Rory snapped on the porch light. Wondering what he was doing here and who the woman was, she opened the front door, still holding the shotgun.

"We need your help," Devlin said, the desperation she heard in his tone cutting straight to her heart. Maybe it was foolish to believe anyone could tell the truth from a few kisses, but she trusted him. Whatever he was hiding, he would tell her when he was ready.

At least that's what she assured herself as she put down the shotgun. "Please, come in." The woman appeared to be shivering, her face taut with fear. "Come back to the kitchen. I'll make some coffee. Or do you prefer tea?"

"Tea, please," the woman said as Rory led them to the back of the house and offered them seats at the table.

She set water to boil on the stove before turning to face the two.

"Thank you," Devlin said, his gaze locking with hers.

Rory felt the full impact of that gaze. She'd run out on him back at Stanwood. And yet he'd brought this woman here because he believed Rory would help.

"This is Anna Pickering. She was a friend of my mother's," Devlin said. "She has reason to fear for her safety at Stanwood. I didn't know where else to bring her."

Rory could see that Anna had been crying and still looked

terrified. "You are safe here," Rory said, taking the older woman's hand. Anna's fear seemed to subside a little.

Devlin gave her a grateful smile. "Anna witnessed my mother's murder back in our homeland. She fears the killer knows she saw him—and can identify him."

Rory felt the jolt at heart level. She'd lost her baby sister and both of her parents so she knew the pain he must be feeling. What must it be like to have your mother murdered—and know who had done it?

"You must go to the authorities," Rory said.

"That's not possible." Devlin seemed to hesitate. "The person who Anna saw is Prince Broderick Windham, the princess's husband. Anna would never live long enough to testify against him."

Rory dropped into a chair at the table, too shocked to speak for a moment. "What can you do?"

Devlin shook his head and she saw the fury just below the surface. "While Broderick killed her, we don't know who ordered the murder. That order could have come from the king himself. Until we know…"

Rory feared what he planned to do even before he said it.

"I must go back to Stanwood," Devlin said. "Are you sure about Anna staying here? I promise I will resolve this quickly and come back. But first I have something for you."

He reached inside his jacket and withdrew a thick file. As he handed it to her, she saw the neat lettering on the tab: Buchanan File.

Her gaze flashed to his. "You went back for this for me?" She could not have been more touched if he'd fought a dragon. "Thank you."

"I hope you won't have to use it. I will do my best to keep the prince from bothering you again, but I didn't want you coming away from the ball tonight without what you'd come there for."

She'd gotten more than she'd hoped out of the ball, as it had turned out. Her only regret was that she hadn't gotten to dance with Devlin, she realized.

"I'll put these away," Rory said, needing a minute. Getting up, she walked down the hallway to her bedroom. She was still touched that he'd done this for her, but concerned how he planned to keep the prince from bothering her again.

She laid the papers on the top of her bureau and turned, surprised to find he'd followed her. The next thing she knew, she was in his arms. It seemed so natural she couldn't have said whose idea it had been.

The kiss, though, had been his. Of all his kisses, she thought she liked this one the best. She found herself melting into his arms, never wanting this to end or his arms to let her go. Who said there were no heroes anymore?

She wanted to cry out when the kiss ended. "You're in danger, aren't you?"

"I have managed to put us all at risk," he said with remorse. "I should never have brought Anna here, but I had nowhere else to go."

"You did right. I will make sure she is safe."

His gaze caressed her face. "You are an amazing woman. I feel as if…"

"You don't know how you've lived this long without me."

He laughed. "I do feel like I know you."

She felt her face heat. He knew her *intimately.*

His gaze held hers for the longest time. "I have to go. Are you sure—"

"Anna will be fine."

He smiled at that. "It's you I was concerned about. I saw

someone watching you from the shadows as you left Stanwood tonight. While I don't think he recognized us, he saw the two of us together. He saw me kiss you."

Rory thought of the tracks around her house, the wire cutters in the shrubs outside her bedroom window and shuddered. "Did you get a look at him?"

"It was a sheriff's deputy."

Rory swallowed a curse. "Don't worry about Deputy Griffin Crowley," she said calmly, although she was furious. How dare Griff spy on her and Devlin. "The deputy and I are old friends. I'm sure he was just concerned about my safety. I saw him in the ballroom. I think he saw me, too." He must have followed her outside.

Devlin didn't look reassured. "If you need me, call Stanwood and ask for Lord Nicholas. He is a friend. He will see that I get the message. In the meantime, I think it best if no one knows Anna is here."

Rory couldn't have agreed more. Devlin said goodbye to Anna, and Rory walked him to the door. She was still fuming about Griff's spying on her—and she was worried about Devlin.

"Are you sure it's safe for you to return to Stanwood?" she asked, once they were outside on the porch.

"I have no choice." He cupped her cheek and kissed her softly on the mouth, making her ache for more. "Be careful. I will come back as soon as I can."

She watched him swing up into the saddle. He seemed to hesitate, as if there was something more he wanted to say. But he didn't. He reined his horse around and, leading the other horse behind him, rode off toward Stanwood.

Rory had the strongest feeling that she should warn him not to go. She started to call after him, but felt Anna's hand on her arm.

"We will pray for his safety," Anna said, joining her.

"He *is* in danger, isn't he?"

"Devlin is like his mother, strong, determined."

"I shouldn't have let him go."

Anna chuckled. "Nothing could have stopped him. Not even you." As they stepped back into the house, the woman seemed to study her openly. "You should rest. When was the last time you ate something?"

Rory couldn't recall. She felt as if she was fighting the flu. "I'm really not hungry and I don't want you waiting on me. Please, you are my guest."

Anna patted her arm. "You must eat and I must keep busy."

JULES ARMITAGE felt his cell phone vibrate and checked the display. Adele Brown. For a moment, the name didn't register. He'd gone back to the ballroom, hoping to see Princess Evangeline and have a word with her.

The phone vibrated again. Stepping out of the ballroom, away from the music and noise, he snapped open his phone. "Hello?"

"I know it's late, but I'm a night owl and you said to call the moment I remembered. Rory Buchanan."

"What?"

"Rory Buchanan. That's the woman who won All-around Best Cowgirl that year, the one you asked me about. I knew I'd remember."

Jules couldn't help being surprised since he'd heard that name mentioned before. Wasn't that the person who was refusing to sell to the princess? But he'd just assumed Rory was a man's name.

As he disconnected, Jules wondered what the groom had been doing with the ranch owner. Was it possible the two of them were conspiring against the princess, the landowner holding out for more money and the groom cutting himself in for some of the money?

The evidence was stacking up against Devlin Barrow, Jules thought with satisfaction. He suspected the princess would appreciate knowing all about this. At the very least, she would send the groom back to the homeland. It would serve him right. Jules didn't like how Devlin acted as if he were a noble.

As the head of security stepped back into the ballroom, he noticed that it was almost midnight. Time for the unmasking and the ball would wind down.

He just had to make sure no one got away with any of the royal silver. No small chore.

Jules looked around for the princess. At the stroke of midnight, Princess Evangeline planned to lead the unmasking. So where was she?

The blare of trumpets announced the approaching midnight hour. Still no sign of the princess. Or the prince.

The crowd stilled as the band began the countdown.

Ten.

Nine.

Eight.

The *pop, pop* could have been champagne bottles opening. No one else seemed to notice it.

Seven.

Six.

Jules moved toward the stairs, toward the direction the sound had come from, worried that something had happened to the princess.

Five.

Four.

The princess suddenly appeared at the top of the stairs. A

rush of expectation filled the huge room. Jules stopped, relieved. As long as she was all right…

Three.

Two.

One.

Confetti fell from overhead like falling snow. Champagne corks popped around the room as masks came off and the music started up again for the last dance of the night.

The princess descended the stairs looking elegant, her mask in her hand. As she passed him, Jules noted that she looked paler than usual.

He wondered where the prince was and could only imagine what had kept him from the unmasking. Not just some woman, he thought as he glanced around the room and noticed who else seemed to be missing.

When the princess found out who'd been sleeping with her husband, there would be more than hell to pay.

EVANGELINE had been to enough masked balls that she could have sleepwalked through this part of the night. She smiled and shook hands with guests and moved through the crowd as if she just hadn't made love with the royal family's barrister instead of her cheating, lying husband.

Trying not to be too obvious, she searched the crowd for Laurencia. Not that her companion could be held completely accountable for this fiasco, since Evangeline had orchestrated it. But something had gone wrong and Evangeline planned to know why.

She spotted Lord Nicholas. No sign of Lord Alexis. Or Lady Monique. Laurencia had been ordered to release the Black Widow from the steam room before the midnight hour. No sign of either woman. Evangeline hoped nothing had gone wrong.

What would happen when Lady Monique returned to her room to find Lord Charles passed out in her bed? Evangeline couldn't bother herself with that. The fool would no doubt think he'd slept with Monique. Clearly, that had been his intent—and Monique's—was Monique trying to make Alexis jealous? Or the prince? And where was Broderick?

Evangeline wasn't fool enough to think that her husband had disappeared from the ball without a woman being involved. But what woman?

She was shaking inside, furious and scared, a deadly mix, as she made her departure and the ball wound down. She couldn't wait to get to her suite. The guards bowed as she passed. Fumbling her key from her pocket, she managed to get the suite door open, desperately needing peace and solitude for a few moments.

The night was far from over. She had to get herself composed or—

A cool breeze skittered across the floor of the suite as the door swung open. Evangeline frowned as she stepped in, closing the door behind her. Montana was too cold this time of year for her. She missed lying on a white sand beach in some sunny clime with the rest of the aristocrats.

But her suite was never *this* cold. She glanced toward the French doors and saw that one of them was open although she was positive she'd closed it when she'd left. Just as she was sure Broderick hadn't been back up to the suite since he'd left earlier.

Slowly, she moved toward the balcony, debating if she should call for a guard. To her relief she saw in the blinding moonlight that the balcony was empty.

Stars sparkled in the clear, cold sky. Below, guests were leaving, horses clip-clopping away as they drew carriages to where the guests could pick up their vehicles. The bright colors of the costumes and the sprinkling of lights around the grounds reminded her of all her hopes for tonight.

Evangeline turned in disgust, closing the balcony doors behind her as she stood just inside, studying the room. Someone had been here. A burglar?

The expensive artwork was where it had been when she'd left the room earlier. Her husband's expensive watch was where he'd dropped it on the side table.

Her gaze went to her desk. She'd had the antique desk brought over from the palace at home at no small expense. It was her favorite since it had belonged to more generations of Wycliffe women than she could count.

She let out a cry of horror as she saw that the bottom drawer had been pried open, the lock broken. Rage washed over her as she grabbed the drawer handle and pulled it open, already knowing what had been taken.

Her anger and horror over the marred desk turned to fear. Those papers in the wrong hands…

She slumped into her desk chair and tried to calm herself. Who had taken the documents? And what was she going to do now?

This deadly game she'd been playing was about to end. And badly, she feared.

The knock at the door startled her. "Yes?"

Jules stuck his head in. "Your Royal Highness."

"What is it, Jules?" she demanded irritably.

The head of security seemed to hesitate.

"What?" she demanded.

"It's the prince," he said, stepping in with a bow. "He's been shot. He's…dead. The deputy is demanding to see everyone downstairs."

Chapter Eleven

The voices in the dining room carried along the hallway to where Princess Evangeline had stopped.

"I was locked in the steam room!" Evangeline would recognize that whine anywhere. Lady Monique. "I could have been *killed.*"

"Don't look at me," Lord Alexis said, clearly disgruntled. "I spent the night looking for you."

Evangeline heard the suspicion in Alexis's voice. While he didn't mind betraying his mistresses, he apparently didn't like it happening to him, she thought with a smile as she continued on down the hallway.

Everyone turned as the princess entered the room and rose to curtsy or bow. Evangeline motioned them back into their seats with a dismissive wave.

"Someone locked me in the steam room tonight," Monique complained, clearly suspicious of everyone at the table.

Evangeline raised an eyebrow. "I'm so sorry. I'm sure the door must have just stuck. I'll see that it's checked at once."

"Is everyone who had access to the second floor here now?" asked a man in uniform. Evangeline vaguely remembered meeting him during the ball. She'd made a point of inviting the local law, Deputy Griffin Crowley who was apparently filling in for the Sheriff.

She glanced around the room but before she could speak, Monique said, "Where's Charles?"

"Charles?" the deputy echoed.

"Lord Charles Langston, the royal family solicitor," Evangeline said.

"Someone find him, please, and get him down here," the deputy said. "You're sure he hasn't left the property?"

"No one has come in or out the front gate since you instructed us to close it," Jules said.

"And you are?" the deputy asked.

"Jules Armitage, head of security."

The deputy nodded, then quickly dismissed Jules. "Your Royal Highness, I assume you've been told about your husband?"

"That he's dead." Evangeline didn't have to fake the trembling in her fingers as she dabbed at her eyes. "There must be some mistake."

"I'm afraid not. Your husband was found shot to death."

Evangeline raised her gaze to the deputy. "Who found him?"

"I did," Lord Alexis said. "When I was looking for Lady Gray, I stumbled across his body in the extra suite across from yours."

Evangeline couldn't hide her surprise.

"Any idea what he was doing there?" Deputy Crowley asked, no doubt seeing her surprise.

"Apparently, he had planned to meet someone there," Alexis said and shot a look at Lady Monique Gray.

"You know anything about this?" the deputy asked Monique.

"No, I told you. I was locked in the steam room the entire time. If Lady Laurencia hadn't found me and let me out…"

She wiped at her own tears as she gave a trembling smile to Laurencia, who sat across from her. "Why don't you find out who locked me in there," she demanded, glaring at the people around the table.

A few moments later, Lord Charles Langston stumbled into the room. He looked hung over and appeared still half-drunk. He dropped into a chair and said, "What's this about Broderick being murdered?"

"*Now* is everyone here?" the deputy asked.

Evangeline glanced around the room. "Not quite." She'd never thought there would be an ideal time to say this, but she'd been wrong, she realized.

"Yes?" the deputy prompted.

"Prince Devlin Barrow Wycliffe isn't here."

A murmur circled the table. Evangeline gauged the surprised faces. No one looked more shocked than Lord Nicholas, the man who'd sponsored Devlin as a groom for Stanwood. Was it possible he hadn't known? That no one had known except her father and Clare Barrow? Until recently, that was.

The deputy was frowning at her. "There's another *prince* here?"

Evangeline nodded gravely. "Indeed there is. Only this one is a *royal* prince by birth."

DEVLIN HAD TIME TO THINK on the way back from Rory Buchanan's ranch. He saw everything much clearer now that he knew about his lineage.

It was no coincidence that he'd been allowed to come to the States to work as a groom on the princess's Montana estate.

Evangeline had known who he was. Which meant that when Lord Nicholas had come to her on Devlin's behalf, she had seen through the ruse at once. How she must have enjoyed letting the two men think they were deceiving her when all the time Devlin had played right into her hands.

It was Evangeline who had secreted Anna Pickering away to Montana. Devlin saw now that Anna had been the bait to get him to the States. To get him to Montana.

Her purpose, though, was still a mystery. Had she planned to get rid of him as she had his mother? While Broderick may have been the one to perform the deed, Devlin was sure the order to kill his mother had come from Princess Evangeline. Or the King, his own father.

So why was he still alive? Or had Evangeline tried to kill him that night in the meadow when Rory Buchanan had saved him?

Once Evangeline discovered the drawer broken on her desk and the papers missing, she would have to move forward whatever plan she'd concocted.

Devlin knew returning to Stanwood could be suicide. But it was the only way he could protect Anna—and now Rory. The deputy had seen both him and Rory on the second floor. Devlin was certain now that it was him Evangeline wanted. He would face her and end this.

With all his heart, he wished it a lie. If only he could convince himself that the birth certificate was a forgery. But had it been, his mother would still be alive. All these years she had protected him from the truth. So what had changed to bring this to light?

There'd been a rumor that the king wasn't well. Devlin had heard talk that Prince Broderick, while he couldn't take the throne, was next in line to rule the country.

That was reason enough for the prince and princess to want all evidence of a true prince in line for the throne to be destroyed.

And yet Devlin had found both a copy and the original of his birth certificate. The copy was now hidden in the stables.

The original at Rory's ranch. What had Evangeline planned to do with them?

What hurt the most was that none of this had been necessary—his mother's murder, the deception to get him to Montana. He had no aspirations to be prince, let alone king of his country. His love was of horses, the outdoors, not politics.

He had to find a way out of this.

But first he had to know who had ordered his mother killed. Princess Evangeline? Or her father, the king?

Lost in his thoughts, at first he didn't see the soldiers. They came out of the pines, the moonlight making them ghostlike as they rode toward him.

It wasn't until they surrounded him that he saw they had their weapons drawn.

EVANGELINE STUDIED Devlin's face as he came through the door and into the dining hall. He expected the worst, she thought with amusement. But even so, he looked determined to face it, reminding her of her father. *Their* father.

Devlin Barrow had their father's blue eyes and handsome features, but he'd gotten his dark hair from his mother. The combination was very pleasing. An acid drip of jealousy made her stomach queasy. How she would have liked it if Devlin Barrow had never been born.

Or that, like his mother, he was dead and buried.

But her father already suspected her of having something to do with Clare Barrow's death. If anything happened to Devlin…

She motioned the soldiers away, then rose to her feet and curtsied to her brother. Half brother. Hating that he'd gotten the better half in both looks and gender.

"I present His Royal Highness Prince Devlin Barrow Wycliffe, son of our king," Evangeline announced.

Devlin's shocked expression alone was worth this moment, she thought. Not to mention the shocked expressions of the others around the table, including the deputy.

"Are you saying…" the deputy began.

"Devlin is my half brother. I brought him here for his protection." Evangeline held out her hand, inviting Devlin to join them. "As you might have heard, there is unrest in our homeland. Devlin's mother was murdered. My father felt it best that his only son come to live in the States, where I could make sure he was safe."

The deputy looked skeptical, but nothing like Devlin himself.

"I'm afraid this is all news to me," Devlin said. "A word, Your Royal Highness?"

"Could you give me a few moments with my…brother?" Evangeline asked. "I feared this news would come as a shock to him. I'm sure he has questions."

"*I* have questions," the deputy snapped. Just then the state police and coroner came through the door. "I want each of these people questioned separately," he said to the officers. The deputy shot a look at Evangeline. "Both of you are next. You have five minutes."

Evangeline gave Devlin a nod, then turned and headed for a private room down the hall. She knew he would follow.

DEVLIN CLOSED THE DOOR behind them. "What the hell is going on?"

The princess seemed taken aback. "How quickly you become the royal prince of the manor."

If what she'd said was true and the papers authentic, then he didn't need to be careful around her any longer and she knew it.

"Why don't we sit down," she suggested.

"Why don't you tell me what's going on?"

She waited a moment for him to sit as ordered. He didn't.

"I thought I made myself perfectly clear out there," Evangeline said finally. "But I suspect it didn't come as a complete surprise. You were the one who broke into my desk tonight, weren't you?"

All of this was coming at him too fast. "What is this about Prince Broderick being murdered?"

The princess shrugged. "I'm told he was shot and killed." She seemed to be taking her husband's death very well.

Devlin knew how the princess operated. For her to announce his lineage, she would have a very good reason. But right now, he was more interested in his mother's killer. "I want to know who killed my mother."

"Don't you already know that as well? I understand one of our housemaids is missing. Anna Pickering? Didn't she tell you that Prince Broderick killed your mother?" Evangeline smiled. "I see that she did."

Now it was finally starting to make sense. Devlin let out a humorless laugh. "You're hoping to pin Prince Broderick's murder on *me?*"

She raised an eyebrow. "You have to admit, you do have the most to gain. Everyone knows Broderick hoped to one day take the throne in my stead. He was ambitious to a fault and clearly acted on his own. It would be understandable that you would want to revenge your mother's death once Anna Pickering told you Broderick killed your mother. And with him gone, you have paved the way straight to the throne on my father's death."

Devlin shook his head. This was just as he'd feared. Just as Evangeline had feared as well. If the king recognized him as his son, then Devlin would be in direct line for throne. His mother had some noble blood. At least as much as Prince

Broderick. That meant Devlin was nobility. His father hadn't been a commoner as he'd always believed.

But Evangeline would never allow him to take the throne and they both knew it. "A murderer could never take the throne."

The princess smiled. "That is true. If you killed Broderick—"

"You know I didn't kill anyone, but that's not going to stop you from trying to frame me for his murder."

"You give me more credit than I deserve," Evangeline said.

Heart sinking, Devlin remembered that he hadn't had time to get rid of the copy of the prince's costume he'd hidden in his cottage. He'd played right into the princess's hands.

"I'll swear the documents are forgeries. My mother wouldn't lie to me. What about my other birth certificate that has me the son of a commoner?"

"Destroyed, unfortunately," Evangeline said.

"My mother wouldn't have lied to me. I will swear to that."

"As if your word would carry any weight," she said, disgusted. "Your mother had no choice. She did it to protect you."

"And the king? Did he also keep it a secret to protect *me?*"

Evangeline frowned at his sarcasm. "You would have to ask him." Her gaze seemed to soften. "I am told your mother was the love of my father's life. His father, King Roland the First, forbad it. I do believe allowing his father to force him into marrying my mother was our father's greatest regret."

Was what she was saying possible? When he'd seen his mother with that sad, faraway look in her eyes, he'd always thought it was because she missed the man she'd married and lost. Now he knew no such man had existed. And since there had been no one else in his mother's life, that could only mean that the pain he'd seen in her had been for Devlin's father, the man who had spurned her for another—and forced her to lie about her own son.

"It does not matter what happened in the past," Evangeline was saying. "You have now been acknowledged as the son of a king, a prince."

"Sorry, but I'll pass."

She laughed at that. "I would think you would be pleased to learn that you are of royal blood. The title comes with both wealth and privilege, which you have had little of in your past."

He could argue that. He'd loved growing up at the stables with freedom, the love of his mother and security—even if false. "The timing of this title you have bestowed on me is a little questionable, don't you think? Trying to kill me failed so you decided to kill two birds with one stone—so to speak—and frame me for Prince Broderick's death."

The princess looked puzzled. "Did you say someone tried to kill you?"

"As if you didn't order it."

"When was this?"

"The first night I arrived. Remember the drink I had in your main parlor? It was drugged and I was lured into the woods where someone took a potshot at my horse."

The princess rose from her chair and rang for a drink, her expression one of fury. "This drug? It made you feel as if you were hung over? Lack of memory? Confusion? And yet full of desire?"

"So you're familiar with it," Devlin said, not bothering to hide his sarcasm.

"You remind me so much of our father."

He doubted she meant that as a compliment. A servant arrived with her drink and quickly left.

Evangeline turned with glass in hand to look at him.

"I'm familiar with the drug because of my husband," she said. "I believe he used it on women."

Devlin stared at her, hating that he felt sympathy for a woman he knew had done much worse than Broderick in her life.

"What happens now?" he asked.

"I guess that will be up to the deputy." She took a sip of the drink. He noted that her hand shook. "Unless you can produce an alibi for the time of the murder…"

Devlin had two alibis—Anna and Rory. But he could use neither. If he did, he would be risking both of their lives.

RORY WAITED FOR WORD from Devlin. News of Prince Broderick's murder swept across the county like a range fire.

"You don't think Devlin…"

Anna shook her head, but Rory wasn't convinced. She recalled how upset he'd been when he'd left. She'd waited anxiously for word. All Georgia knew was that the state police had been called in and that Deputy Crowley was busy with the investigation.

"There are lots of rumors circulating," Georgia told her. "I was scared to death you'd done the prince in."

"I never saw the man," Rory told her, but then remembered she *had* seen him in the ballroom. Worse, she'd been seen herself on the second floor balcony with a man wearing the same costume as Lord Broderick.

As the days passed and still no word from Devlin—or a visit from the deputy—Rory thought maybe Griff hadn't recognized her the night of the ball.

Apparently, from what she'd heard, he was restricting his questioning to the guests and princess since no one else had been allowed on that floor the night of the ball. Not even servants.

But the biggest news by far was that a *second* prince had

been on the grounds the night of the ball. The prince was being questioned in Prince Broderick's death.

Rory waited for word from Devlin as to what was happening next door. She grew more antsy as the weather turned as it so often did this time of year. It began with rain, long dark dreary days.

As the temperature dropped, the rain turned to sleet, leaving the yard and Rory's pickup coated in ice. Finally, it began to snow with a vengeance, blanketing the ranch with a foot of the cold white stuff.

Rory had always liked snow. It signaled the end of one season and the beginning of a new one. She didn't even mind the cold mornings, taking the wagon out to feed the cattle.

But she'd sold off the cattle, and between the flu bug she couldn't get rid of, making sure Anna was safe and worrying about Devlin and what was happening with the murder investigation, she didn't have the energy to leave the house anyway. Fortunately, there wasn't much to running the ranch this time of year other than keeping the horses fed and watered.

With Prince Broderick's murder, the offers on her ranch had stopped as abruptly as they'd started. She knew she should feel relieved since Devlin had said he would take care of it. No wonder she found herself waiting for the other shoe to drop.

Had she felt better, she might have at least checked to see if any more of her fence had been cut. But she really wasn't up to that, either.

She wondered if this was delayed grief over her parents' deaths. She'd been so busy trying to save the ranch, she hadn't had time to grieve.

The weather and worry left her with a strange melancholy. If it wasn't for Anna, Rory feared she would have fallen into a deep depression. Anna had insisted on doing all the cooking.

Probably after having one of Rory's meals. Now Rory was eating too much and still didn't feel all that well. Although she ached to see Devlin.

A few times over those dark and depressing weeks, she noticed tracks in her yard again. She kept the doors locked now and the curtains drawn even in daylight with Anna there. But some nights, Rory swore she could sense someone just outside. If she let her imagination run away with her, she could hear him breathing against her window pane.

Sometimes she pretended it was Devlin. That he stood out there wanting to knock, but wouldn't allow himself to.

Rory had no knowledge of the strange world he lived in. For all she knew his visa had come due and he'd been forced to return to his birth country.

And yet she sensed that he was still just miles from her. Within reach if only she could reach out to him.

"I'm worried about you," Georgia said the last time she was out to the ranch house. "Are you sure you're feeling better?" Georgia was the only person who knew about Anna. And Devlin.

"I'm fine. It's just this time of year." Winter, once it started, lasted for months in this part of Montana. This year, Rory didn't feel up to it.

"You should come in for my knitted stocking class next month," Georgia suggested. "It's a really easy pattern."

In the past, Rory would have laughed at the suggestion. It was odd. The thought of knitting suddenly had a strange appeal.

That was when Rory knew she probably needed help. Maybe she'd schedule an appointment with her doctor. Her stomach roiled. When was this flu ever going to run its course? Maybe she had an ulcer. She blamed it on nerves.

Rory only half listened as Georgia filled her in on all the Whitehorse gossip. A Texas family named Corbett had bought the old Trails West Ranch, Arlene Evans was now a grand-mother—and was dating of all things, and their mutual friends Maddie Cavanaugh and Faith Bailey might both be coming back to town, possibly to stay.

"Are you sure you're all right?" Georgia asked.

She pushed away her coffee, the smell making her ill. "I'm fine."

"Maybe you should see a doctor," Georgia said before she left.

"I'm *fine,*" she'd protested and walked her friend to the door. She barely made it back inside to the bathroom before she threw up—and finally admitted that she didn't have the flu.

THE NEXT DAY, Rory called Georgia and asked her to come out. "Would you mind staying here with Anna while I go into town?"

Her friend had been happy to agree. Rory knew she could have asked Georgia to pick up what she needed as Georgia had done over the past few weeks.

But this was something Rory wanted to handle on her own. Also, she hadn't been out of the house in days and thought it might make her feel better to get out.

She knew she was being paranoid, but she had the strang-est feeling she was being followed even though every time she looked back, she didn't see anyone.

At the drugstore, she purchased several pregnancy tests, again feeling as if someone was watching her. It was embar-rassing enough checking out, especially in a small town where everyone knew everyone's business.

It was also the reason Rory hadn't asked Georgia to buy the tests for her.

Back at the ranch house, Anna was doing what she was always doing, cooking or cleaning, keeping busy.

Rory showed the tests to Georgia, then quickly went into the bathroom to confirm what she already had accepted.

"Oh, Rory," Georgia said as she saw Rory's face when she came out of the bathroom. "It's definite?" she whispered even though Anna was in the kitchen with the radio on and couldn't hear them.

Rory could only nod.

"I suppose I don't need to ask—"

"It's the groom's." Devlin Barrow's baby.

Georgia hugged her friend. "Oh, sweetie. You've fallen in love with your groom?"

All Rory could do was nod numbly.

"You have to tell him," she said as they sat down in the living room.

Anna had built a fire earlier when she'd gotten up. The woman seemed to feel the need to be busy, rising early each morning. The flames licked at the logs, a soft popping sound filling the room.

Rory had thought about nothing else since she'd realized she was pregnant. She hadn't needed the test. She'd known, the way women had always known.

"You have time to decide what to do," Georgia said.

Rory smiled at her friend. The decision had been made the moment she'd finally admitted she was pregnant. "I'm having this baby."

"Shouldn't you discuss this with the father first?"

"He isn't a factor in my decision," Rory said. "He can't be. He's not even a U.S. citizen. For all I know he's been sent back to his country."

"Rory—"

"I know what you're going to say."

Her friend had tears in her eyes. "It's just that I know you.

I've seen you struggle the past four years trying to hold on to the ranch. Once you make your mind up about something…"

"I know it's been a losing battle," Rory said, hating that everyone had been right. Especially Griff. "It's been impossible to let go, though."

"And now with a baby…"

Her hand went to her stomach. She thought of the life growing inside her. "I'm going to sell the ranch." As hard as the words were to say, Rory knew it was the only thing she could do now.

"Are you sure?"

Rory couldn't help but laugh at her friend's expression. "All this time, you've encouraged me to consider selling and now you're worried that I'm making a mistake?"

"Not a mistake. It's just that I know what this place means to you. Won't you resent that you had to sell?"

"I want this baby," Rory said with a rueful smile. "Part of the reason I clung to the ranch was that it was all I had left of my family."

"You are going to tell him, aren't you?"

Rory nodded. "But only because he has the right to know."

"Good." Georgia sounded relieved.

"There isn't going to be a happy ending here, you know."

Georgia shrugged with a wry grin. "I can hope, can't I?" Her expression changed to one of horror. "Oh, God, what happens when Griff finds out about this?"

"Griff is the least of my problems." Rory was worried about what would happen when Devlin found out about the baby.

Anna came in with warm peanut butter cookies from the oven and a pitcher of milk.

"At least Anna will see that you eat like you're supposed to," Georgia said after Anna had left the room. "You don't think she knows, do you?"

DEVLIN HAD BECOME A PRISONER at Stanwood. He was never without guards.

"It's for your own protection," the princess had told him.

He was also not allowed to leave the country because of the murder investigation. He had little doubt that he would be arrested soon. Unless he produced an alibi for the night of the ball. He had to make sure both Rory and Anna were safe from any repercussions before he could do that.

So far the deputy had told him not to leave Montana.

So he waited for the chance to escape and return to Rory's ranch. He'd dreamed about her every night and worried about her safety and Anna's. To keep himself sane, he'd thought about Rory's ranch house with its rock fireplace, its warm rugs on the hardwood floors, its history.

When Rory had talked about her ranch, he'd heard her love for her home. He missed his home although he'd known he'd never return to Barrow Stables, but he'd thought he would return to his country. Now he knew that wouldn't be possible.

Even *with* alibis, Devlin worried the evidence was stacked against him—and his alibis were both questionable anyway, since one had been his lover—and the other was now his mother's friend, a woman presumed missing.

He no longer wanted to return to his homeland. That had become the past, one of cherished memories of his mother and nothing more. He wasn't fool enough not to realize the danger he would be in the rest of his life as the royal prince in line for the throne in his country.

Devlin had hoped to talk to Lord Nicholas. They'd had only a few words together without being interrupted. He suspected that was the princess's doing. But yesterday Nicholas had managed to get him a quick message.

"Be ready in case there is a fire on the estate," Nicholas had said.

Devlin hadn't understood his friend's meaning. But tonight as he heard the commotion, he saw the blaze in one of the cottages closest to the palace and knew. As the alarm went out, Devlin saw that his guards seemed confused as to what to do. When they finally realized they had no choice but to leave their posts and fight the fire, Devlin slipped out.

When he reached the stables he was none too surprised to find a horse already saddled, waiting for him. He swung up onto the mount, thoughts of Rory driving him forward.

He rode hard, snow blowing up as his horse's hooves churned across the frozen expanse. He breathed in the fresh air, feeling free for the first time in weeks.

As he glanced back to make sure he hadn't been followed, Stanwood rose out of the pines, illuminated by the blaze of the groom's cottage. He half hoped the whole place would go up in flames and put an end to Stanwood.

But he knew the princess would rebuild something even more ostentatious, cold and impersonal.

By the time Devlin reached the Buchanan Ranch it was late. No lights burned from behind the curtains.

He hid his horse in the barn and started toward the house, willing himself not to run although his heart urged him to. He couldn't wait to see Rory and now he was so close…

Through the pines, he could see the snowcapped Bear Paw Mountains and Little Rockies rising from the prairie floor to pierce the huge dark sky.

He suddenly missed his homeland, missed the familiar smells and foods and people. Missed his mother. They'd worked together for years, been best friends.

Devlin had hoped to one day give her a daughter-in-law to

love as a daughter. Had hoped to give her grandchildren. That made him clench his jaw as he recalled one of his last discussions with his mother. Had she been trying to warn him?

She had encouraged him to wait for the right woman. "There is no hurry. The right one is out there. Wait for her."

Now, knowing what he did about his birth father, he knew she feared he would marry and produce an heir to the throne. She had protected him for more than thirty years. He'd been safe. As long as he didn't produce an heir before Princess Evangeline did.

He closed his eyes and cursed the king under his breath. His father. The king would have been only a prince when Devlin had been born. Was it possible his mother had been in love with Prince Roland Wycliffe? Or had the man forced himself on her?

Devlin blew out a breath, thinking of his own one-night stand with Rory. He wanted her just as desperately tonight. More so.

He warned himself that the timing was all wrong. Would always be all wrong. Now that he knew who he was.

As he neared the house, he ached at the thought of what he must do. He had to tell her the truth.

Devlin started as the door flew open. Rory ran out, barefoot, the ends of her robe flapping in the breeze. He caught her, picking her up, laughing in spite of himself, their breaths coming out in icy white puffs.

"I knew you would come," she whispered against his ear as he carried her inside and set her down.

"I would have come sooner if I could have." He touched her flushed cheek, warning himself not to kiss her. This was hard enough. "So much has happened. There's so much I need to tell you."

She pressed a finger to his lips and shook her head, then kissed him softly before she took his hand and led him through the dark house.

RORY HAD AWAKENED TO A SOUND. Instantly, she'd been afraid it was her Peeping Tom outside. But her heart had begun to pound, and she'd found herself flying out of the bed, grabbing her robe as she'd hurried to the door, knowing even before she'd opened it that it was Devlin.

They moved quietly past Anna's bedroom, the older woman snoring loudly enough to be heard even through the closed door.

Rory led him to her bedroom at the back, closing the door behind him.

"We have to talk, Rory," he said. "There is something I must tell you."

Something she must tell him, too. But not now.

Just the sight of him standing there after these many days of worrying, all she wanted was to be held in his arms.

"Please," she whispered, her gaze locking with his. She saw his eyes fill with something akin to love. Or lust. Right now it didn't matter.

He swept her up, kissing her, burying his hands in her hair as he drew her against him as if she was the first breath he'd taken in days.

He peppered her with kisses as his hands moved along her curves, a soft groan escaping his lips before he found her mouth again.

In a flurry, they kissed, tugging at clothing as if in silent assent that they wanted nothing between them tonight.

Naked, they stood clutching each other, movements slowing as their gazes touched. Rory looked into his eyes and saw

the emotional war raging there. The one thing she knew fo
certain is that she didn't want to hear what he had to tell her
Any more than she wanted to tell him her news.

Tonight, she just wanted him. Nothing more. She kissed
him, brushing her lips across his. He caught her up in hi
arms again and gently laid her on the bed, lowering himsel
beside her.

"Rory." He breathed her name like a promise. Or a curse

She raised up on an elbow to brush his dark hair back from
his forehead, just as she had done that first night.

His dark blue eyes flashed with a need as strong as breath
ing. He cupped her head with his hands and drew her down
his mouth capturing hers, their bodies melding in the heat o
passion and this all-consuming need for each other.

Chapter Twelve

As the sky began to lighten, Devlin lay spent; Rory snuggled into the curve of his shoulder. He knew she wasn't asleep and hadn't been for some time.

Devlin didn't want to be the one to break the sated silence between them. He wanted to stay right there, in the big old iron bed, photos of cowboys and favorite horses on the rough walls of the old ranch house.

For weeks he'd been living in the palace, been treated like a prince. He'd hated every moment of it.

He knew what he wanted. But because of the blood that coursed through his veins, he thought it would always be denied him.

He had to tell Rory the truth. The sun would be rising soon. He had to return before he was missed. If he hadn't already been missed.

"There's something I need to tell you," she said.

"Please, let me go first." Whatever she had to say to him, he couldn't hear it. Not until she knew the truth about him.

He drew away from her, getting out of bed and pulling on his britches.

Rory sat up in the bed, looking worried. At a sound at the window, she turned quickly. He saw her expression.

"What is it?"

She shook her head. "Nothing. It's just that I had a Peeping Tom. I'm sure it's just the wind."

He glanced toward the window, thinking if anyone was out there, it would more than likely be royal soldiers come for him. But he didn't like the idea that someone had been hanging around the ranch. At least Anna was here with Rory now, although that didn't relieve his worries about either woman's safety.

"I'm sorry," Rory said. "There was something you needed to tell me."

Devlin nodded solemnly. "The night of the ball, you asked me what I was doing in the princess's desk…"

"And you said you'd have to kill me if you told me."

"What I should have said was that telling you would put your life in danger," he said. "Now your life is in danger because of me anyway and I have no choice but to tell you for your own safety." He hurried on before she could stop him. "I found a document in the bottom drawer of that desk. It was my birth certificate. My *real* birth certificate—and the reason my mother was murdered."

He expelled a breath. "I'm the son of the king, a prince, the prince in line for the throne of my country."

It took a moment for the words to register. "You're a *prince?*" Hadn't Georgia told her that there had been a *second* prince at the ball that night? Someone who was being questioned for the murder of Prince Broderick?

"I had no idea," Devlin was saying. "Even when I saw the birth certificate…" He sat down on the edge of the bed beside her. "You have to understand. I hate this."

"You're saying you have to go back and rule your country?"

"No. It's not that simple," Devlin said.

No, it wasn't simple at all. Rory thought about what she had to tell him. The words froze in her throat. If Devlin was a prince, heir to the throne, then what did that make the baby she was carrying?

The light tap on the door made them both start.

"Yes?" Rory's voice broke as she swung out of bed and away from Devlin. She'd thought she was getting a groom, but he'd turned out to be a prince—and she was devastated by the news. Something was definitely wrong with this fairy tale.

"I have made breakfast," Anna said. "It is almost light. Devlin must return as soon as he has eaten. I have made his favorite."

Rory reached for her clothes, not surprised Anna had also heard Devlin's arrival last night. Apparently Anna also knew more about Devlin Barrow than Rory did.

"Wait, I can't leave you like this," he pleaded.

"There isn't anything else to say. You're a prince and you will be returning to your country." The irony was that she'd fallen in love with a groom and been completely content with that.

The sky was lightening. Shafts of silver filtered through the curtains. Rory dressed quickly and hurried out to the kitchen, avoiding Devlin's gaze as well as his grasp.

Anna glanced back at her; her gaze shifted to something over Rory's shoulder as Devlin followed her into the room. The older woman seemed to study the two of them. She didn't look happy.

"I need to talk to Devlin," Anna said as she slid a plate onto the table.

"I'll go check his horse," Rory said and grabbed her coat from the hook, disappearing out the back door before Devlin could stop her. Before she let the painful tears reach her eyes.

But not before she'd smelled the sausage Anna had cooked Devlin for breakfast. She hadn't gone two feet out the back door before she was sick to her stomach.

THE THIRD TEST was also negative. Evangeline dropped the testing equipment into the trash can with a curse and gripped the sink, her fingers aching from the pressure. She had failed miserably. Her dreams of returning to her homeland with the next king were shattered.

She was alone, childless, banished to this alien country. For the first time, she let herself break down. It was early, the servants wouldn't be coming up for another hour. And she was alone, able to finally let it all come out.

Huge shuddering sobs racked her body. The pain poured out of her, years of it, until the sobs slowed and she realized she was crying for Broderick. For what could have been between a husband and wife.

Evangeline wiped her tears, pulling herself together. Broderick was a bastard. Now a dead bastard. All she had to concern herself with at present was the arrest of Devlin Barrow Wycliffe for Broderick's murder. Two birds, one stone, she thought.

She had taken care of the threat, but she had failed to produce an heir. Without an heir, all was lost. Her father would never let her return home.

The thought paralyzed her. She'd never taken her fate lying down. She'd always fought back, going after all she wanted. How could she give up now?

At thirty-six, there was little chance of remarrying now that word of Broderick's murder was out. Even with Devlin convicted of the crime, there would be those who would never elieve she hadn't done it. She would be seen as a woman as espicable as Lady Monique. A Black Widow.

No noble worthy of producing an heir to the throne would ant anything to do with her. Few ever had. At her age there as little chance she could produce an heir even if there had een a man willing to chance suffering the same fate as roderick.

The husband of a princess was little more than window ressing. Evangeline suspected Broderick hadn't realized that— ntil he'd married her. He'd wanted more. Most men would.

The princess ignored the knock at her door. She didn't ant to see anyone. Especially Laurencia. She'd made a point f avoiding the woman since she'd heard Laurencia had taken her bed as soon as the deputy had questioned her. Appar- ntly she felt some guilt for the prince's demise. Probably ecause she hadn't gotten Broderick to the right bedroom the ight of the ball.

Had Broderick come to Lady Monique's room, been icked into bedding Evangeline…

The princess pushed the thought away. Broderick was dead nd she wasn't pregnant. Evangeline no longer had any nterest in how she'd ended up in bed with the wrong man.

The knocking became more insistent.

Evangeline checked herself in the mirror and went to the oor, looking forward to the tongue-lashing she intended to ive whoever was standing there.

"Your Royal Highness." Jules Armitage quickly bowed. "I ust speak with you. It is a matter of utmost urgency."

"Whatever it is—"

"You will want to hear this, Your Highness." He lowered is voice so the guards at the end of the hall didn't hear. "It oncerns Devlin—*Prince* Devlin."

"You wouldn't dare speak evil of the son of the king, would you?" she demanded.

Jules met her gaze. "I serve you, Your Highness. The true heir to the throne."

Evangeline studied the little man for a moment before she stepped back and motioned him into the suite, closing the door firmly behind him.

DEVLIN STARTED AFTER RORY, but Anna stopped him. "I have to go to her. Can't you see? She's ill."

"Do you not see what is wrong with her?" Anna demanded in a hushed tone as she drew him away from the door.

"I told her about the birth certificate I found in the princess's bottom desk drawer. She is sick because of who she thinks I will become."

Anna frowned impatiently at him. "Rory carries a child. It is morning sickness that makes her ill. Trust me, I know such things."

Devlin looked toward the back door, feeling as if she'd stuck a fork in his throat. "Who is the father?" When Anna didn't answer, he glanced back at her and saw her expression. *"Me?"*

"Can you not tell by how angry she is with you?" Anna demanded.

His mind raced. Was this the news she had meant to tell him? And had changed her mind when he'd told her his news? The impact of that revelation finally hit him.

Rory was carrying his child. He thought *he'd* be sick. "Anna, she can't be pregnant. Not with *my* child. If Evangeline should find out…"

Anna shuddered, wrapping her dimpled arms around herself as if to chase off the chill. "She wants this baby."

"She can't have this baby," Devlin said and heard his pain registered in his voice. *His* child. His child with a woman he'd fallen in love with. And yet, this baby couldn't be born. Not now that he knew whose blood ran through his veins.

"She thinks because I am the bastard prince I must return to our homeland to take the throne. She will change her mind about keeping the baby."

Anna shook her head. "She is strong and determined and in love with you. She will not give up this baby—not at any cost."

Devlin cursed under his breath. "Princess Evangeline is trying to frame me for her husband's murder." The older woman didn't seem surprised. "You and Rory are my alibi, but I can't tell the deputy about either of you—especially now. You must make her understand. If Evangeline finds out Rory is pregnant with a possible heir…"

The back door opened on a gust of cold snowy air. Rory stood silhouetted against the dawn. "Your horse is ready and I just saw the deputy's patrol car headed this way. Also I found fresh footprints outside my bedroom window."

"HAVE YOU TOLD THE DEPUTY about this?" Evangeline asked when Jules Armitage had finished.

"No, Your Highness. I wanted to speak with you first."

"And you are sure you saw both Prince Devlin and this Rory Buchanan on the second floor outside my suite?"

"Yes. I will swear to that."

She thought about the trouble Broderick had had purchasing the Buchanan Ranch. "You say they met before that night?"

"In an old line shack on your property. They were intimate, Your Highness," he said, clearly reading that was what she most wanted to know.

"Lovers?"

He nodded.

She remained still even though her insides were in turmoil. If Devlin and this ranchwoman were lovers on his first night in Montana… "Is there more?"

Jules nodded. "I believe Rory Buchanan is harboring your missing servant, Anna Pickering." He took a breath, no doubt knowing how the next news would affect the princess. "I also have reason to believe that Rory Buchanan is with child. Prince Devlin's child."

RORY WAITED back in the kitchen, fighting not to breathe in the sickening smell of sausage. Anna was now hidden upstairs in the attic.

"You must trust Devlin," Anna had said before going up. "He is a good man. He will make the right decision about the future."

"He's a real prince."

"Yes," Anna agreed, missing Rory's sarcasm.

Now Rory heard the slamming of a car door in front of the house. She braced herself for the worst. Footfalls on the porch, then pounding on her front door.

Let this not be about Devlin.

She stood and went to open the door to the deputy.

"You're up early," Griff said the moment he saw her dressed and wide-awake at the door.

"Griff." She glanced at her watch. "Is something—"

"Are you alone?"

She blinked as his question sunk in. "What?"

He pushed past her. "I asked if you're alone."

"Yes," she snapped. "Why would you ask?"

He was standing in the middle of her living room. The county deputy sheriff. And yet she felt an odd sense of unease.

He turned to look at her, anger in his expression. "The last time I saw you, you *weren't* alone."

She frowned. Had he seen her with Devlin earlier?

"The night of the ball," he supplied. "I saw you on the second floor balcony with a man."

"You were *spying* on me?" she demanded, going on the offense.

He wasn't fazed. "I checked. You didn't have an invitation to the party."

The smell of fried sausage unfortunately still wafted in the air. Rory tried to hold down the nausea as she faced the deputy. "Why would you care whether or not—"

"Surely you've heard. Prince Broderick Windham was murdered the night of the ball."

"What does that have to do with me?"

Griff was looking toward the kitchen. "You've already had breakfast?"

"Why? Are you hungry? I think there's some sausage left."

"I didn't come out here for breakfast," he snapped.

"Well, then, I don't understand what you're doing here." She feared she understood only too well. Devlin had gone back to Stanwood after learning that Prince Broderick Windham had killed his mother. Devlin would have told the deputy where he'd been at the time of the murder when he gave his statement, wouldn't he have? So why was Griff asking her about this?

"What were you doing at the ball?"

She stared at him. "You don't think I killed the prince, do you?"

"You said you were going to take care of your problem with your neighbors yourself."

"Not by killing some stupid prince."

"You were *there*."

Rory couldn't believe this. She didn't feel well and had to sit down. "I went to get copies of the offers made on my ranch so I could prove harassment just like you suggested."

Griff took off his Western hat to rake his fingers through his hair in obvious agitation. "I didn't think you would *break* in to get them."

"I didn't break in. I crashed a masked ball. I don't believe that's a criminal offense."

He slapped his hat back on his head. "I know what a hothead you are. You threatened me with that shotgun you keep by your back door just the other day."

"I said I was going to get my shotgun. That's not the same as threatening you with it."

"You were on the second floor where the prince was killed," Griff shouted at her.

She cringed and he lowered his voice.

"What were you doing with that man? How is it you even know him?"

So he had seen her and Devlin together. Or Devlin had told him. "I'm sure Devlin told you how it happened. As I said, I was there for the offers on my property."

"I asked how it is you knew him?"

"I don't really know him." It was her first lie. "We just crossed paths." That at least was true. And if you were a person who believed in fate…

"And the night of the ball was the first time you'd met him?"

"What does this have to do with the murder?"

"Prince Devlin Wycliffe Barrow is the number one suspect in my murder case."

Rory took the news badly. "He didn't kill anyone."

"And you know this how, since you barely know the man?"

She shook her head. All this was coming at her too fast and

he smell of sausage was making her sick. "I was with him. I'm his alibi."

The moment she said it, she saw Griff's expression and knew Devlin hadn't told him. Why wouldn't Devlin have told him that he was with her and couldn't have killed Broderick?

"Why wouldn't he have mentioned that he was with you?"

"I don't know. Maybe to protect me."

"A woman he barely knows?" the deputy asked sarcastically.

"I'm telling you the truth."

"All I have is your word that you were with Prince Devlin at the time of the murder."

"My word has always been good enough before," Rory said, her anger growing. Griff had been spying on her at the ball. He knew damned well she hadn't killed anyone. He also knew she hadn't been alone on that balcony.

"You have any other guns in the house besides the shotgun?" he asked, all business now.

"You know I have my father's guns, but I keep them locked up."

"Let's see 'em."

She couldn't believe this was happening. Getting to her feet, she led him to her father's den. His gun cabinet was against the wall. She reached on top of it to take down the key. Opening the old-fashioned pine gun cabinet, she stepped back so Griff could get to the contents.

The deputy had pulled on latex gloves, she saw. Fear made her weak as she watched him rummage in the cabinet, pulling out several of her father's pistols.

He sniffed the barrel end of the .45. "When was the last time this was fired?"

She shook her head.

"I'm going to have to take this to the lab."

Rory could only stare at him. He didn't really believe she
would shoot someone. This was about her turning down his
marriage proposal. That and Devlin. He'd seen her with
Devlin. Had he also witnessed the kiss?

She thought of Anna in the attic and prayed Griff wouldn't
do something crazy like insist on searching the house. Rory
was all set to demand a search warrant.

"I'm going to need you to make a statement as to your
whereabouts the night of the murder."

"I can come down to the station as soon as I change."

His gaze took her in.

She was feeling a little green around the gills.

"No need. We can do it here."

She would have much preferred meeting him at the station
away from the house—and Anna. But she also didn't want to
make him suspicious by insisting on going into town to the
sheriff's department.

She watched him bag her father's .45, then had her sign that
she'd allowed him to take it. The whole thing seemed ridiculous, but she said nothing as he pulled a small tape recorder
from his pocket and set it on the coffee table in front of her.

"You look pale."

"I'm fine," she said noticing the way he was looking at her.
"I don't think my early breakfast agreed with me."

He looked at her as if he knew she was lying.

But there was nothing he could do about it. And she wasn't
about to tell him what was really going on with her.

"Tell me everything," Griff ordered, officious again and
clearly angry as he snapped on the tape recorder. His gaze
locked with hers. "And I mean *everything*."

Rory had the horrible feeling that Griff knew everything
already. Or at least a lot of it. Devlin had told her that the

deputy appeared to have been following her the night of the ball. Did he just want to hear it from her? Then what?

Griff's cell phone rang. He cursed, checked the screen, then cursed again. "I have to take this." He shut off the tape recorder, rose and stepped out onto the porch.

Rory watched him from the window. Whatever news he was getting, Griff seemed to be upset by it. When he finished the call, he placed one.

She'd expected him to come back in when he finished. Instead, he walked to the porch railing. She saw that he was gripping the top rail, his knuckles white from the pressure.

Rory glanced toward the stairs, all her instincts telling her to get Anna out of there, and fast. But the older woman wouldn't be able to go far in the snow on foot even if she knew which way to go.

Maybe if she hid in the barn—

The front door opened and Griff came back in. She noted his face was flushed, his eyes appearing red-rimmed.

"I have backup on the way," he said in a calm voice that belied the look in his eyes. "I know you have been harboring a criminal." He glanced toward the stairs. "Anna Pickering is wanted as an accomplice in the murder of Prince Broderick Windham. Along with providing Devlin Barrow with inflammatory information about his mother's death, she also gave him detailed information about the palace."

"Anna had nothing to do with Broderick's death and neither did Devlin," Rory snapped. "Someone is trying to frame her."

"Frame her?" The deputy snorted. "Just like someone is trying to frame Devlin Barrow? Excuse me. *Prince* Devlin Barrow Wycliffe." He must have seen her expression. "Proof has been found that implicates him as well as Anna Pickering."

Griff stepped toward the stairs and Rory instinctively moved in front of him to block his way.

He glared at her, his eyes as hard and cold as obsidian. "Either get her down here or I'll go up and drag her down and arrest you for aiding and abetting. Your choice, Ms. Buchanan."

Chapter Thirteen

At the sound of sirens, Rory went upstairs to get Anna. She knew Griff would make good his threat although Rory wasn't worried about herself, but Anna. She'd seen something in the deputy's eyes that had warned her he could be cruel to Anna to get back at Rory.

Anna and Rory waited downstairs with one of the state investigators as Griff and the others searched the house and the grounds. Rory couldn't imagine what they were looking for. Devlin? Or proof that he'd been there?

When they returned to the living room, though, Rory could tell from the deputy's displeased expression that he hadn't found what he'd hoped for.

"We're taking Anna Pickering in now," Griff said and ordered the investigators to cuff her.

"Is that really necessary?" Rory demanded. "I doubt she is capable of overpowering you since she isn't half your size."

Griff shot her a warning look, but told the man to forget the handcuffs. "I'm not through with you," he said when the others had gone out to the patrol cars. "Don't leave. I'll be back. I still need a statement from you."

Rory said nothing as she watched him go. All she could

think about was that, according to Griff, Devlin would be arrested for the murder of Prince Broderick Windham. She remembered what Devlin had told her about who to call if she was in trouble.

She hurried to the phone and dialed Lord Nicholas Ashford's cell number. It rang only twice before he picked up.

"Nicholas," he answered.

Rory could hear a racket in the background. "It's Rory Buchanan. I'm—"

"I know who you are."

"They've arrested Anna Pickering as an accomplice to the prince's murder," she said quickly. "The deputy sheriff said they were going to arrest Devlin—"

"They already have," he said. "The royal guards are holding him until the deputy sheriff gets here."

She choked back a sob. "He didn't kill anyone. He was with me the whole time or Anna when Prince Broderick was killed. Surely once he tells—"

"I'm afraid that information would only put both you and Anna in more danger," Nicholas said. "You must trust me. I'm doing everything I can to help Dev. Right now he is only worried about you."

"I'm fine." She didn't take Griff's threat seriously. Even if he did arrest her for aiding and abetting alleged criminals, Rory knew once she told Judge Randall her side, he would throw the case out.

Unfortunately, the judge couldn't help Anna or Devlin, not with them both facing murder charges.

"I have to go," Nicholas said. "I'll tell Devlin you called and that you're safe."

"Tell him I…" Fortunately, Nicholas had already hung up before she had the chance to make a fool of herself.

"YOUR SISTER SENT ME," Charles Langston said as he glanced into Devlin's small cell block, nose wrinkled.

"The last person I need help from is my...sister or her father's barrister," Devlin said, not bothering to get up from the cot where he sat. He was more worried about Rory and Anna than himself even though Nicholas had assured him that Anna had been taken into custody and Rory had said to tell him she was fine.

"Princess Evangeline insists," Charles said as he looked around for a place to put down his briefcase. "I'm sure you'll want to know about the evidence against you at this point."

The barrister found a stool and dragged it to the front of Devlin's cell. "Now, let's see. Motive. According to the princess's statement to the deputy sheriff, Anna Pickering had informed you before the ball that Prince Broderick had murdered your mother and had made an attempt on your life as well."

The royal attorney took a breath and continued. "Opportunity. You were seen on the second floor wearing a costume like the one Prince Broderick had worn the night of the ball. The head of security has testified as much and the costume you wore was found in your cottage. Apparently the seamstress had made copies of the original design as per the princess's request in case of any accident prior to or during the ball."

Evangeline had thought of everything, Devlin realized.

Charles looked up at him. "All that seems to be missing is the weapon. Deputies are searching the grounds as we speak. The princess is sure the gun will be found."

"I'm sure she is." Devlin got up from the cot to move to the bars, wishing he could reach through them and get his hands around the attorney's neck. "I'm sorry, other than to let me know that the princess has me right where she wants me, what is your purpose for coming here? I know it isn't to help me."

"You're wrong," Charles said indignantly. "The princess says she will ask for leniency for you to keep you from the death penalty. She also," he rushed on before Devlin could comment on that, "asked me to tell you that the head of security is in possession of evidence that you met one—" he checked his notes "—Rory Buchanan at a small cabin on your first night at Stanwood and again the night of the ball, if not on several other occasions, for the purpose of driving up the selling price of her ranch and thwarting Prince Broderick's attempts to buy said ranch."

Devlin gripped the bars. "That's a damned lie."

Charles didn't even blink. "The princess wanted me to inform you that she would be willing not to take action against said Rory Buchanan. She also would consider helping clear Anna Pickering so that she might be sent back to her homeland to be with her family."

Devlin stared at the man. "In exchange for what?"

RORY CALLED GEORGIA CRYING. "He's a prince," she blurted out the moment she heard her friend's voice.

"Rory?"

"Devlin. He's the prince. The other one. The one who's not dead."

"Sweetie, what are you talking about?"

"Devlin told me. He's going to be king. He's…" She couldn't stop crying.

"I'm coming out to the ranch. Don't move. I'll be right there."

True to her word, Georgia arrived only minutes later. By then Rory had gotten control of herself.

"Hormones," she said as she opened the door and felt herself tear up again at just the sight of her friend.

Georgia hugged her and led her over to the couch. "Now what is this about Devlin?"

"He's a prince. He found his real birth certificate. He's the son of the king and in line to the throne."

"He's that *other* prince we heard about?"

Rory nodded.

Georgia's eyes lit up. "You're in love with a prince? You're having a baby with a prince? Why are you crying?"

"I don't want to be in love with a prince. I don't want to have a prince's baby. I wanted a groom who would stay here on the ranch with me and our baby."

She'd said it. Her fairy-tale fantasy. And Devlin had gone and ruined it all by being a prince who would be a king. "He has to go back to his own country to become the king. I really don't want to be married to a king." She teared up again. "Why couldn't he just be a groom?"

Georgia laughed and took her hand. "Do you realize how many women would love to find out the man they love is a prince? I'm sure the two of you can work something out. You told him about the baby, right? Oh, Rory, you didn't. Why not?"

"I couldn't and now he's been arrested for Prince Broderick's murder. Griff saw the two of us together. I told him that Devlin couldn't have done it. That he was with me at the time of the shooting."

"He thinks you're covering for Devlin."

Rory nodded. "Anna's been taken into custody as well and charged with aiding and abetting Devlin."

"Oh, no." Georgia seemed to hesitate. "Griff doesn't know that you're pregnant yet, right?"

Rory shook her head.

"I think that's good. Sweetie, Griff seems a little too obsessed with you."

"He'll just have to accept it."

Georgia didn't look convinced. "I hope so."

"He's just jealous, but I'm afraid he'll use it against Devlin and Anna."

Georgia nodded. "I'm more afraid he'll use it against you."

"I can handle Griff."

"I hope so. Rory, you have to tell Devlin. He needs to know everything if he hopes to defend himself against these charges."

"WHAT DID PRINCE DEVLIN SAY?" Evangeline asked when Lord Charles arrived at Stanwood after coming straight from the local jail.

"He denied everything."

She smiled. "I'm not surprised."

"He asked what assurance you could give that you wouldn't go back on your word."

Evangeline laughed. Her bastard brother was no fool. He clearly had taken after their father.

"I believe he suspects you plan to use Broderick's murder as a way to get the Buchanan ranch and get rid of him and Rory Buchanan," Charles said. "He says he wants no title nor does he aspire to the throne."

"Everyone wants to be king and have all that that entails," she snapped angrily. "He will change his mind when my father dies."

Charles shrugged. "How shall I proceed?"

"Hire him a lawyer. A good one, but not too good." She waved her hand through the air. "That's all."

Evangeline waited until Charles left before she rose to pour herself a drink. She needed to take the edge off, but she never drank to excess. Control was as essential as breathing for her.

For the first time in weeks, she felt as if she finally had the situation in hand.

Turning at a sound behind her, she was shocked to find Lady Laurencia standing in the middle of the room. Had she not heard the knock? Or had the woman simply walked in without being acknowledged?

"What are you—"

"I came in as Charles left," Laurencia said.

Evangeline was taken aback by the impatience she heard in her friend and companion's tone. Nor had Lady Laurencia curtsied or greeted her as was custom.

The woman looked awful, her face puffy, eyes red.

The princess said as much, assuming this explained her friend's rude behavior.

"I just came from the doctor."

"You're ill?" This, Evangeline thought, would give her the perfect excuse to send Lady Laurencia back to their homeland— and out of her sight.

Laurencia straightened, her gaze locking with the princess's. Evangeline had only an instant to realize that something had changed in her companion.

"I'm pregnant."

Evangeline stared at her, wondering why she hadn't seen it. The weight gain, the times Laurencia had seemed weak and ill. Evangeline had thought her a malingerer.

"Pregnant?" This silly nit was having a baby out of wedlock when Evangeline had to go to extraordinary levels to attempt to get pregnant? And when had Laurencia found time to propagate as busy as the princess had kept her?

"Yes, pregnant," her companion said, her look almost challenging.

"Who is the father?" Evangeline couldn't imagine. Someone back in their homeland because, on closer observation, Laurencia appeared to be fairly far along.

"Don't you know?"

Evangeline was tired of whatever game Laurencia was playing. "Just tell me," she said with an irritated, bored sigh. "Or don't. I suppose this means you'll want to return home."

Laurencia didn't answer but walked to the window, her back to the princess. "That's up to you."

"I'll make the necessary arrangements for you to return," Evangeline said, glad to have it settled. She didn't like this Laurencia and thought it must be hormones. Otherwise the woman would have known better than to disrespect the princess, let alone to flaunt her pregnancy.

Laurencia would be useless pregnant anyway. Evangeline would find herself taking care of her companion instead of the other way around.

"You might want to reconsider," Laurencia said, smiling as she turned to face her again. "I'm carrying the next heir to the throne."

For a moment, Evangeline thought she had to have heard wrong. "You're carrying Devlin's child?"

Laurencia laughed. "Devlin? The bastard prince?" She shook her head. "No, I'm pregnant with Broderick's baby."

The floor seemed to collapse under Evangeline. She grabbed the back of a nearby chair. "You're lying."

"This from the woman who threw me at her husband?"

Evangeline would have gone for Laurencia's throat had she not felt so ill herself. "How dare you speak to me—"

"Why don't you call a guard? Or shoot me like you did Broderick. Or…we can make a deal."

Evangeline stared at her. She'd rather rip the woman's head off than make a deal with her. How long had she been playing her? Obviously for months and all the while sleeping with Evangeline's husband.

"A deal?" the princess repeated.

"You need this baby I'm carrying. The doctor confirmed it today. I'm carrying a boy."

A male heir. Isn't this what Evangeline had prayed for—for herself? And most feared that her husband would conceive some bastard with one of his whores? She just hadn't thought it would hit so close to home.

"My blood isn't quite as royal as yours, but it's noble enough on both sides of the family and Broderick's. You should be able to pass the baby off as yours."

Evangeline battled through her confusion and anger. "Are you telling me you're willing to sell me an heir to the throne?"

"You can afford it and you really can't afford to pass on my offer," Laurencia said with a chuckle. "I know too well, and just in case you're thinking what I know you are, I took out an insurance policy. If anything should happen to me or this baby... Well, I don't have to tell you how this works. You wrote the book on deception."

"Whatever made me think you were stupid? Or meek? Or loyal?"

"I *am* loyal. I'm the best friend you've ever had although you always treated me more like a servant," Lady Laurencia said as she placed her hand over her bulging belly. "I'm giving you what you always wanted. An heir to the throne."

"And what am I giving you, Lady Laurencia?"

"I WANT TO SEE THE PRISONER," Rory demanded of the dispatcher when she reached the sheriff's department.

"Neither prisoner is allowed visitors," she said. "Deputy Sheriff Griffin Crowley's orders."

"You tell Griff that I'm going to see what Judge Randall has to say about this if he doesn't—"

"Rory." Griff stuck his head out the doorway from the back of the department. "Send Ms. Buchanan back."

Rory pushed through the swinging gate and down the hallway to where Griff stood waiting for her. His glare didn't faze her. Nor did his threats. She was running on high-grade fury.

"Step into my office," he ordered, opening the door and practically shoving her inside. "I could have you arrested for coming down here, causing a disturbance and threatening me."

"Who's threatening who? If you were going to put me in jail, you would have already done it. You know the princess is behind this. Just like she was behind trying to buy me off my ranch. If you'd let me see Devlin—"

"His lawyer's in with him."

"I'll wait," Rory said, hugging her purse to her as she took a chair across the desk from Griff. "Devlin didn't kill anyone and Anna certainly had nothing at all to do with this."

"So you've said," Griff said, leaning back in his chair, his gaze intent on her.

"Had you let me give my statement, I would have told you about Devlin's alibi." No matter how she felt about Griff at the moment, she'd known him her entire life. He would do the right thing once he understood what was going on. "I was with Devlin at the time Prince Broderick was murdered."

Griff raised an eyebrow. "You'd better tell me everything. How again do you even know Devlin Barrow?"

She told him about the night of the thunderstorm and being trapped in the line shack with Devlin.

"That was the morning I asked you to marry me," Griff said. "I thought you said you were alone?"

Rory couldn't help but look shamefaced. "It wasn't something I was proud of. I—"

"You slept with him?" Griff was on his feet, his voice raised. "You..slept…with…him?"

Rory felt all the air rush from her. "I—"

"Get out."

She stumbled to her feet. "Griff—"

"Get out."

"Let me see Devlin. Let me talk to him."

"Go home, Rory. Haven't you heard? There's a winter storm warning out. You'll be lucky to get home before the blizzard hits."

She'd heard about the storm on the radio coming into town. "Please, Griff. This isn't about you and me. Let me see him."

"No visitors are allowed."

"Don't you mean just me?" Rory demanded.

Griff looked her in the eye. "Especially *you*. At his request. He doesn't want to see you, Rory. Now go home. I'll call later to make sure you made it."

"Don't bother." She turned and left, fighting tears as she stepped out of the sheriff's department into a blizzard. The winter storm had already begun.

Chapter Fourteen

Devlin heard the *whoosh* of the cell block door opening, followed by footfalls as the door clanged shut. If it was that royal attorney coming back with another deal…

Deputy Sheriff Griffin Crowley came to a stop in front of Devlin's cell. "I hope your accommodations are satisfactory. I know you've grown accustomed to living in a palace now that you're a prince."

Devlin ignored the man's sarcasm.

"I just spoke with Rory Buchanan," the deputy said after a moment. "She tells me she was with you at the time of the shooting."

Devlin recalled what Rory had said about Deputy Griffin Crowley being her friend, the two of them having grown up together. "It's true. We were together. We heard what I believe were two shots being fired. The sound seemed to be coming from the next room."

The deputy looked surprised. "Why didn't you tell me that when I took your statement right after the ball?"

"I was fearful for Rory's safety."

The deputy pushed back his hat. "Why is that?"

"I didn't want her involved."

"In Prince Broderick's murder?"

Devlin swore. "I told you. I didn't kill him. Deputy, I have to make bail and get out of here."

"That's not likely since you're a flight risk."

"You don't understand. I can't protect Rory if I'm locked up in here."

"That's real noble. Still, you're facing murder charges. I would think if you had an alibi…"

"I didn't mention that I was with Rory because I was afraid Princess Evangeline would find out."

"What makes it your job to protect Rory from your sister?" the deputy inquired.

Devlin hesitated for only a moment. The deputy was Rory's friend. The man obviously cared about her or he wouldn't have been keeping an eye on her the night of the ball. "Rory's pregnant with my baby."

"*What?*" The deputy scoffed. "I thought you said the first time you were together was on that balcony at the ball—"

"We were together before that. The night of the big thunderstorm back in September."

The deputy's eyes narrowed. "At that old line shack."

How had he known about that? Rory must have told him.

"You can understand now why I'm worried about Rory and why I need your help. Please, you're Rory's friend."

"*Friend?* Is that what she told you? That we're just friends? We're a lot more than that." The deputy smiled and Devlin felt his stomach lurch. "I knew something was wrong with her. Pregnant. With your baby?" The deputy let out a curse as he slammed his fist into the cell door.

Blood spewed across the concrete floor as the man cursed and drew his injured hand into his mouth.

"Rory is mine," the deputy spat. "She has always been

mine. Even when she was engaged to that dumb jackass Bryce. I knew it wouldn't last. All I did was make sure it ended sooner rather than later. Bryce was a fool. He would believe anything you told him."

The deputy had a faraway look in his eye now that frightened Devlin more than his earlier rage. "I waited it out, telling myself that my day would come. Just give her time. Do you know how many years I've waited? Did she tell you I asked her to marry me? Bet the two of you had a good laugh about that."

Devlin had stepped back, fearing that the deputy would open the cell door.

"And now she's pregnant with some foreigner's baby?" The deputy shook his head as if it was all too much for him. "Friends? I couldn't be friends with a woman like that. No," he said. "Rory isn't having some murdering foreigner's baby. I can tell you right now that isn't going to happen."

"I need to talk to my lawyer," Devlin said as the deputy backed away from the cell door.

If the deputy heard him, he gave no indication as he turned and stalked toward the cell block door.

The door *whooshed* open, clanging shut behind the deputy. Devlin stood, too stunned to move for a few minutes, all his fears paralyzing him to the spot.

From behind his small barred cell window, he heard the rev of an engine. In two strides, he was on the cot and looking out the window as the deputy in his patrol car sped down the street in the direction of Rory Buchanan's ranch.

Devlin jumped back over to the cell door, grabbed the bars and screamed for a guard.

"You keep that up and—"

"I will give you a million dollars if you bring me a phone."

The guard blinked. "Like you have—"

"I am Prince Devlin Barrow Wycliffe, the son of a king. Bring me a phone and I will see that you never have to work another day of your life."

The guard licked his lips and looked around the empty cell block. "I suppose it would be all right for you to make a call."

Devlin called Rory at once, but the connection was terrible. He couldn't be sure she'd heard him before the line went dead.

Panicked, he had no choice but to make the second call. Surprisingly, he had less trouble than calling Rory, who was only a few miles out of town.

"Tell him my name is Devlin Barrow Wycliffe, son of Clare Barrow. It is urgent he take my call. A matter of life and death."

King Roland Wycliffe's voice wavered only slightly as he took the phone. "Who is this?"

For a moment, Devlin was at a loss for words. "Devlin Barrow Wycliffe, son of Clare Barrow and King Roland Wycliffe the Second. I'm calling from jail in Montana. I need your help."

OVER THE WIND, Rory had barely heard the sound of the phone ringing. She'd hurried to the phone before she remembered that Griff had said he would call to make sure she'd made it home safely.

Her hand wavered over the receiver as it rang a second time and a third. Finally, she picked it up. "Hello."

"Rory, get out of there now! He's on his way—" The line popped and crackled too loudly for her to make out the rest of his words.

"Devlin?"

No answer, the interference on the line growing louder and then nothing.

"Devlin? *Devlin?*" He was gone. Worse, she feared the line had gone dead. The blizzard outside. Often the phone went out, snow taking down the lines. The power often failed as well in a storm of this magnitude.

It had been Devlin. But where had he been calling from? The jail? Or had he gotten released?

She hung up, picked up again, planning to call the jail. No dial tone. The line was dead.

She tried to remember his exact words before they'd been disconnected. *You have to get out of there.*

Out of the house?

He couldn't have meant that. Not in the middle of the worst blizzard of the year. What kind of sense did that make?

He's on his way...

The urgency she remembered in Devlin's tone more than the words had her glancing toward the front of the house.

He's on his way...

A chill rippled over her skin. She reached for her coat and truck keys, going on nothing more than faith. It had been Devlin. He'd been trying to warn her. But warn her about whom?

The wind whirled snow around her in a blinding funnel of cold white as she stepped out onto the porch. She could barely see her pickup parked only yards away. A snowdrift had formed around it. She'd pay hell getting out her road and when she reached the county road, the drifts could be even worse.

For a moment, she hesitated, the warmth of the house calling her back along with her common sense.

The urgency and fear she'd heard in the voice on the phone forced her down the steps. The snow was deep and getting deeper by the moment. She plowed through it to the pickup and jerked open the door, slipping a little on the running board as she climbed in.

Once behind the wheel, she dug her keys from her coat pocket. Her fingers trembled from the cold inside the pickup ıs she found the right key and stuck it into the ignition. The ɛmperature had dropped drastically.

She thought of her parents. They'd gone off the road in a ɔlizzard only four years before. Because of the lack of traffic ɔn roads in this part of Montana, they'd been trapped in their ɛar until a snowplow had discovered them.

Even with extra clothing, some food and water her mother ıad always carried in the winter, they'd died. Frozen to death ʌhen the temperature had plummeted, their car running out ɔf gas after hours trapped in a snowdrift.

Going out in this weather could be suicide. But staying…

Rory turned the key in the ignition. Over the howling wind ʃhe heard a click. She tried again. The pickup had always ʂtarted, even in the dead of winter. Had to be one of the battery ɛables again. She tried once more, then picking up the wrench ʃhe used for this particular problem, she popped the hood ʴelease and climbed out into the storm again.

Breaking through the drifts to the front of the pickup, she ʴaised the hood, her breath coming out in white puffs, her ʲingers and toes already cold and aching. She couldn't wait ʇo get the pickup going, turn on the heater and—

As she reached in with the wrench to tap the battery cable ɛonnection, she froze. The battery was gone.

DEVLIN COULDN'T BELIEVE IT when the guard came back into ʇhe cell block, this time carrying the keys.

"You have some mighty powerful friends," the guard said. 'The governor himself called to say we had to let you go. I ʇold him the deputy sheriff in charge wasn't here right now ınd he said I was to get my ass down here and let you out ʴight away. So…"

Devlin waited anxiously as the guard put the key in the

lock. There was a clank and the door groaned open. Devlin was out in an instant.

"I'm going to need a car. Any car. I'll pay," he said to the guard.

"Pay how much?" the guard asked warily.

"Give me the keys to whatever you've got. I'll pay you twice what it's worth. Three times as much. Just give me the damned keys and your gun."

"My gun?"

"Come on."

The guard dug out his keys and handed over his weapon, looking dazed. "The governor didn't say anything about giving you my keys or my gun."

"Where's your car parked?" Devlin asked as he tucked the pistol into his jail-issue pants and covered it with his shirttail.

"It's that old blue pickup outside the front door. It ain' worth much, but it's got four-wheel-drive and you're going to need it if you're planning to go anywhere in this storm."

The last of the guard's words were lost to Devlin as he borrowed a coat and ran out of the sheriff's department and into the storm.

The pickup was right where the guard had said it would be. The engine turned over on the first try. Devlin shifted the truck into Reverse and backed out.

He knew which way to go since he'd seen the sign to the Buchanan Ranch when he was taken from Stanwood in the patrol car.

The deputy had a head start. Worse, Devlin couldn't be sure that Rory had gotten his message. If she hadn't, she would open the door to the deputy, still believing she had nothing to fear from him.

Devlin drove through the blowing and drifting snow toward the ranch, praying he'd get there in time to save Rory. And their baby.

RORY SLAMMED THE HOOD and glanced down. The snow had drifted, obliterating all tracks. Was whoever had taken her battery still here on the property?

She had to assume so. Someone didn't want her leaving.

She moved around the side of the pickup, gauging the distance between her and the house. Her tracks had already filled in from where she'd tromped through the snow to reach the truck.

The wind swirled the snow around her in a cold, blinding whiteout. She could barely see the house let alone tell if someone was waiting for her on the porch.

Her shotgun was hanging by the back door. Her only hope was reaching the house, getting the gun—

She took an exhausting step toward the house, then another, plowing through the blowing snow. The cold seeped into her bones. Fear already had her chilled. She sought anger, hoping to fuel her for what she had to face.

She was almost to the house when she was struck by a feeling so intense she stopped to spin around, knowing she was about to come face-to-face with—

There was no one there. Just snow and cold and wind howling eerily off the eaves of the house. But the feeling that she wasn't alone was still with her, so strong it made her skin dimple with goose flesh. She stumbled as she turned and practically ran the rest of the way to the house.

The porch appeared empty as she darted up the steps, across the worn wood and grabbed open the door. The wind caught the storm door, ripped it out of her hand and slammed it against the house.

The glass shattered, tinkling into a million pieces onto the cold porch floor.

Rory had her hand on the knob of the large wooden door behind it and was shoving the front door open, stumbling in as she hurried to get the door closed and locked behind her.

She knew he was probably in the house waiting for her but she had to try to get to her shotgun. Even with the gun, she didn't have great odds since she had no idea what she was up against.

The shotgun held two shells. That meant she would have two chances. But without the weapon, she'd have no chance.

Running on adrenaline and fright, she looked down the dark hallway toward the kitchen and the back door. Even as she reached for the light switch, she knew her power line was out. Either down because of the storm or cut like her phone line.

The suffused white light from the storm bled in through the windows, ghostlike.

Rory could see the kitchen wall and the shape of the shotgun on its rack by the back door. Between her and the shotgun were the doors along the hallway.

If he was in the house, he was probably hiding in one of the rooms off the hall. Waiting to grab her as she passed. She couldn't shake the feeling that he'd been watching her for weeks. Maybe even longer. Waiting for this day.

Every fiber in her wanted to run down that hallway to the shotgun, but the wood floor was slick under the snow-coated soles of her boots, forcing her to walk.

She kept her gaze on the shotgun, all her hopes pinned on it as she walked. The only sound was the squeak of the snow eneath her boots and the blood rushing to her head. Just a ew more feet.

Rory passed the first door, then the next, her nerves on dge. At the sound of a gust of wind blowing snow against he kitchen window, she jumped and had to get control of erself again.

She couldn't panic. Not yet, anyway. As she stepped into he large ranch kitchen, she couldn't hold herself in check any onger. She sprinted to the back wall, grabbed the shotgun nd spun around, knowing he was there. Had been there all long.

He was.

Chapter Fifteen

Deputy Griffin Crowley stood in the kitchen doorway, silhouetted against the light of the storm. "Easy, it's just me."

Rory swallowed back a scream, relief making her weak, the shotgun in her hands suddenly too heavy. She let it slump down against her thighs as she took a shaky breath.

"You scared me. I thought…" She shook her head. What had she thought? She was just so relieved that it was only Griff.

"Someone took my battery out of my pickup," she said. "My phone went dead and the power is out. I think the lines have been cut."

"Who would do that?" Griff asked.

"The Peeping Tom."

"I thought you were so sure it was one of your royal neighbors?"

Griff hadn't moved and while she couldn't see his features in the dim light of the storm, she felt a pang of disquiet. His body language seemed all wrong. So did his tone of voice.

She'd just told him that someone had taken the battery from her truck, possibly cut her phone and power lines, and it was as if he hadn't heard her. The same lack of real concern he'd

hown when she'd told him about someone sneaking around
er place, cutting her barbed-wire fence.

"What are you doing here, Griff?" Her voice broke.

"Don't you need me, Rory?"

"Yes, but…"

"You only need me on *your* terms, isn't that right? But I've
lways been here for you, Rory. When Bryce left town, I was
ere. I tried to help you then, but you weren't having any of
t, were you, Rory?"

Her fingers tightened on the shotgun, but she tried not to
nake any quick movements. Devlin's urgent words on the
hone. "You have to get out of there. He's on his way—"

Griff? Is that who Devlin had tried to warn her about?

"I did everything I could," Griff was saying. "I thought
nce you realized that you couldn't run this place without
ne… I figured once you knew someone had been around the
lace, cutting your fence—"

"You cut my fence?" Her heart slammed against her
hest. She swallowed back the bile rising in her throat and
ried to breathe.

Griff took a step toward her. "I just wanted you to see that
ou needed me."

All this time it had been Griff. The wire cutters in the
hrubs outside her bedroom window—they'd been his? She
ad a flash of a memory of his pocketing the tool. He'd said
e hadn't wanted her to see it, to protect her, but he'd been
rotecting himself.

A mixture of fear and revulsion threatened to drown her.
he took a step back, remembering the broken shrubbery
vhere someone had stood and looked in her bedroom window.
Deputy Griffin Crowley.

She was going to be sick. Why hadn't she seen it before?

Rory willed back the wave of nausea and lifted the shotgun pointing it at him.

"What are you going to do? Shoot me?" Griffin asked. H sounded more hurt than worried.

"You've been stalking me?" Her voice cracked.

"You had to have known how I felt about you."

She shook her head.

"I asked you out after you and Bryce split up. I thought yo just needed time. But it turns out you just needed a princ instead of a deputy."

"I want you to leave," she said motioning with the shotgun "I mean it, Griff. I don't want to shoot you, but I will."

He took a step toward her. "I'm not going *anywhere*. I'v waited for you and waited for you. Now I'm going to tak what I should have had a long time ago."

She felt her blood turn to ice as she flipped off the safet on the shotgun and pulled the trigger.

A loud click filled the kitchen. Alarm rocketed through he Griff had removed the shells.

He snatched the shotgun from her hands and threw it acros the kitchen. The gun crashed into the cabinet, wood splinter ing. His palm smacked the side of her face with a stingin blow, the sound of the slap filling the silence.

She ducked as he tried to hit her again and he knocked he to her knees. His hand threaded through her long hair. She le out a scream as he dragged her across the kitchen floor an down the hallway toward her bedroom.

"Griff, no! Please!"

He stopped and spun on her. She cowered on the floo afraid he would hit her again. Instead, he knelt next to he jerking her head up by her hair so that their faces were onl inches apart.

"I told myself you couldn't shoot me," he said, spittle and inking breath hitting her in the face. "Rory couldn't kill me. ot the man who has loved her all these years, the man who is been here for her whenever she needed help. But I thought st to be safe, I'd take the shells out anyway. You disap-inted me, Rory. And now you're going to make it up to me."

He tightened his hold on her hair and jerked her off alance. She was sliding on her back now as he dragged her own the hall to her bedroom doorway.

Rory fought to get her feet under her. Her hands clutched the walls, the edge of the bedroom door frame, anything to eep this from happening. She had no illusions about what he anned to do to her.

Hurt her. Hurt her in the worst possible way.

"Griff, for God's sake, please. Don't do this. I'm sorry if hurt you. I had no idea how you felt."

They had reached her bedroom. He let go of her hair to kick e door closed. The only light in the room was that coming through the curtains from the storm.

Rory scrambled to her feet, frantically looking for some-ing in the room that she could use as a weapon.

But Griff was on her before she could take a step. He osed one large hand around her neck and forced her down the bed. She dug her fingers into his forearms, fighting to ke the pressure off her throat as he held her down.

"Your life is in my hands," he said. "I could kill you ght now."

She said nothing. Couldn't have gotten a word out with his ngers digging into her throat. She clamped her hands around is wrist and pushed as hard as she could, relieving a little of e pressure.

Her gaze locked with his. Tears filled her eyes from the

pain, the horror and the realization that she'd never known th man. Or what he was capable of.

His expression changed. He loosened his hold. "Rory," h said, his voice thick with emotion. "I didn't want it to be lik this. Why couldn't I have been the one you loved?"

His head jerked up as if he'd heard something. She cou see him listening. She did the same, praying someone wa coming. But all she heard was the wind and the sound of ic crystals pelting her bedroom window. No one would be on in this weather. By now the road was probably closed.

Griff let her go, stepping back to her closet, all the tim keeping her in view as he reached in and dug around.

She glanced behind her, desperate for something she coul use as a weapon. Her letter opener was on the desk on th other side of the bed.

She knew she'd never be able to get to it before Gri caught her. Even as he dug around in the closet, he was watch ing her, expecting her to do something. Maybe even hopin she would so he could hurt her some more.

He moved away from the closet with one of the large, wor T-shirts that she slept in. "Here put this on. Nothing else."

She noticed his other hand was behind him as he tossed h the T-shirt. She was shaking so hard, the T-shirt slipped fro her fingers.

"If you can't do it…" He took a threatening step towar her. Oh, God, what was he holding behind him?

"I can do it," she said quickly. She hadn't realized she wa crying until then.

Griff reached toward her with the hand that she could se She flinched. He swore under his breath. "Stop acting lik you're afraid of me," he said as he tenderly brushed a tea from her cheek.

Rory swallowed and tried to stem the tears, but the heaving sobs boiled up from deep within her.

"Don't cry," Griff said softly. "I'm here to help you now. I'll take care of you. I can make this all go away."

His tone was so gentle, she looked up at him. Was there a chance he wasn't going to rape her? She told herself she would agree to whatever he wanted, anything, just to buy time and delay whatever he had planned for her.

She stripped out of her clothing, feeling his eyes greedily on her. Her stomach roiled with fear and repulsion as she slipped the T-shirt over her head, tucking it around her.

Griff smiled at her modesty. "Well, Rory?" he asked as he wiped at her tears, his thumb pad rough against her cheek. But it was the other hand, the one he still held behind him, that sent her terror spiraling. "What's it going to be?"

Rory tried to breathe, the weight against her heart making it next to impossible. She thought of the baby she carried and knew she would do anything to protect it.

"What do I have to do?" she asked meekly, thinking of the letter opener on her desk behind her.

"All you have to do is get rid of that foreign bastard's baby," he said, to her horror. "Don't worry. I'm going to help you."

He pulled his hand from behind him and she saw that he held one of the wire hangers from her closet.

DEVLIN ALMOST MISSED the turnoff to the Buchanan Ranch. Visibility in the blizzard was only a few feet in front of the pickup and the ranch road had blown in.

He'd been busting through drifts all the way down the county road. Now he touched his brakes as he realized he'd missed the turn. The pavement had been warmer than the air when the storm had begun.

Now it was black ice, shiny in the old pickup's headlights. He felt the tires lose traction and begin to slide.

Fighting the wheel, he pulled it out of the slide only to crash into a drift. The pickup spun like a top, careening off the road and into the ditch. Snow flew up over the windshield as the pickup kept going.

When it finally came to a stop, Devlin tried to drive it out, but the snow was too deep, the pickup bogged down, the drift so deep the pickup would probably be there until spring.

He had to put all his weight against the driver's side door to push it open and then fight the snow to reach the road.

Not much time had passed and yet he felt as if he was moving in slow motion as he started down the road at a run.

The deputy had a head start. He would already be at the house. Already be with Rory. *God, don't let me be too late.*

The wind blew the snow horizontally across the road. If it hadn't been for the tops of the fence posts sticking out of the drifts, Devlin wouldn't have known he was even on a road.

He hadn't gone far when he saw the patrol car in the ditch. Only faint indentations could be seen in the snow where the deputy had climbed out and made his way down the drifted-in road.

Through the pelting snow, Devlin caught sight of the ranch house ahead. No lights burned behind the curtains. Maybe Rory had understood his phone call before they'd been cut off. Maybe she'd gotten out in time.

All hope of that died, though, when he saw her pickup nearly buried by a drift in her front yard.

"Rory." Her name blew out in a puff of frosty air. A cry of pain and prayer.

He pulled the weapon he'd taken from the guard and slowed his pace as he neared the house. The front stairs had isappeared in the snow. He stumbled and almost fell as he tepped into the deep snow only to hit his boot toe on one of ne stairs beneath the snow.

Grabbing the railing, he climbed up to the porch, trying to e as quiet as possible even though the wind howled around im like a wounded animal.

No sound came from within the house as he tried the front loor. Locked.

Backtracking, he made his way around to the rear, telling imself if it was locked as well, he would break in through a vindow, do whatever it took to get inside that house.

The back door was unlocked. He let it swing into the kitchen, his pistol ready.

An eerie silence filled the kitchen as he stepped in and closed the door behind him. He was breathing hard. He teadied his breath and his hand holding the gun as he listened.

Voices. He took a step toward the sound of Rory crying, vith murder in his heart.

'GRIFF. NO." Rory scrambled back on the bed. "You'll kill ne." The desk was behind her. Just a few more inches and she would be able to reach the letter opener.

But she knew the letter opener would be useless unless Griff was within striking range. She would get only one chance. She had to make the blow count or she was dead. Griff was too close to the edge of sanity, wavering like a tightrope walker on that thin line.

Once she went for the letter opener, it would push him over, she had no doubt of that. She could only imagine what he would do to her. If she failed, she prayed he would kill her quickly.

Just the thought of the baby she carried almost killed her courage. Maybe she could talk Griff out of this. There had to be another way that she could save her baby. Firing the shot gun at him was different from stabbing the man with a letter opener. What if she froze?

Griff began to unwind the coat hanger, straightened it to horrible point, all the time watching her. She didn't dare move, barely breathed.

His hand grabbed her ankle to pull her toward him.

Rory flung herself backward. Her hand came down on the surface of the desk. She'd underestimated where the letter opener had been. Her fingers brushed it. The cold metal skittered away.

She reared back further, her fingers closing around the blade as Griff's fingers locked on her ankle and jerked her toward him and the edge of the bed.

He was so much stronger than she was. She slid across the bed, banging her head on the edge of the desk as she was jerked toward him.

He laughed as if he'd thought she'd been clutching at the desk, reaching for something to hold on to. His attention was on her naked thighs as he parted her legs, the coat hanger scraping her inner thigh.

She sat up, letting the momentum as he dragged her toward him carry her forward. With the letter opener clutched in her fist, she barely noticed the bedroom door open.

Her arm shot out in a roundhouse swing, the blade of the letter opener catching the light from the storm, as she drove the point into the side of Deputy Griffin Crowley's neck.

Griff looked up. His fingers dug into her thigh. "You ungrateful bitch!"

A scream broke from her throat, filling the air with a high-pitched terrified cry as she felt the clothes hanger pierce her skin

Even the sight of Devlin coming through the door seemed

urreal as if she'd conjured him up out of nothing but air. She watched as if no longer part of the scene as Griff was dragged backward, the tip of the clothes hanger scraping the length of her leg as she screamed in pain and horror.

At the sound of a struggle, she scrambled wildly back on the bed, landing on the floor on the other side, pressing herself against the wall, unable to stop as if the scream had a life of its own.

The boom of the gunshot finally silenced it.

Rory clung to the wall. She could feel blood running down her legs. *The baby. Oh, God, not the baby.*

When a large, dark figure came around the end of the bed, Rory recoiled.

Not until Devlin spoke her name and knelt next to her, taking her trembling body to him, did she finally let the tears come.

Chapter Sixteen

Devlin rode in the front of the snowplow holding Rory wrapped in a quilt. She'd stopped crying but still trembled, her eyes glazed over as if she'd seen something so terrifying it had blinded her.

He could only imagine what had happened before he'd gotten to the ranch house. Her face was bruised, her lip cut, one eye swollen shut.

As he'd wrapped her in the quilt, he'd seen the blood that had run down her leg and the bright red cut that trailed from her inner thigh to her ankle.

It had been all he could do not to put another bullet into that crazy son of a bitch lying dead on the floor.

As the hospital came into view, Devlin saw the state patrol cars waiting for them, light bars flashing.

The moment the snowplow came to a stop, one of the state troopers opened the passenger side door. From inside the emergency room, medical personnel rolled out a gurney. Within minutes, Rory was taken inside.

"I don't want to leave her," Devlin said to the state investigator.

"I'm sorry, but you have a lot of explaining to do," the trooper said.

"Just let me make sure she's going to be all right first, then 'll tell you everything."

Several of the troopers exchanged looks. "We'll go in with ou."

It wasn't until Devlin was assured by the emergency room loctor that Rory's injuries were superficial that he finally let nimself take a real breath.

"What about the baby?" he asked.

"She didn't lose it. But after what she's been through…"

Devlin knew it was too early to know what the emotional lamage would be. Or if she still might not miscarry.

"We're going to keep her here for a few days," the doctor said.

"Can I see her?"

The doctor shook his head. "We have her lightly sedated."

"Would you tell her when she wakes up that I'll be back as soon as I can?"

The doctor nodded and glanced toward the waiting troopers. 'I know Rory Buchanan. She's a strong woman. Little can keep her down."

Devlin hoped the doctor was right about that as he left the hospital with the state troopers.

IT WAS SEVERAL DAYS before Devlin was released and cleared of the two killings—one he had actually committed but only to save Rory's life and that of his child's.

His statement about Deputy Griffin Crowley was supported by what Rory had told the state investigator—and what they found in Crowley's house.

In one room, a large bulletin board was covered with surveillance-type shots of Rory. The photos had been taken from various vantage points around her ranch with a tele-

photo lens. All of the shots had been candid ones take
without her knowledge.

In a drawer at the deputy's house, they'd found evidenc
that he had spied on other residents—just not to the extent h
had Rory Buchanan.

During that time, the murder investigation of Prince Brode
rick had also taken an unexpected turn. Lady Monique Gra
had been arrested.

She had been apprehended trying to leave the countr
Trace evidence of gunpowder residue had been discovered o
one sleeve of her masquerade ball costume. She swore tha
she hadn't killed Prince Broderick, that there was a secon
costume like hers, but no such costume was found.

In the Black Widow's luggage, a .45 pistol had been dis
covered, the same one used to kill Prince Broderick. Appar
ently she'd shot him with his own gun. Lady Moniqu
continued to argue her innocence, saying she'd never fired
weapon in her life and that she'd been framed.

But upon her arrest, investigations were underway in th
deaths of not only her former husbands, but also some of he
now-deceased lovers. Further charges were expected to b
filed in other countries.

Anna Pickering had been released and allowed to retur
home to her country. Princess Evangeline Wycliffe Wind
ham had no comment on Lady Monique's arrest or Ann
Pickering's release. The princess was reportedly holed up i
the palace, sending everyone except her best friend and com
panion Lady Laurencia back to their homeland. Word sprea
that the princess was with child.

The day Devlin was released, a free man, all he could thin
about was getting to Rory. That's why he hardly noticed th
large black car waiting for him outside the sheriff's depar

ent until the back door opened and he saw King Roland Wycliffe waiting for him.

"A moment of your time," the king said and Devlin climbed nto the back of the car next to his father.

RORY HAD BEEN HOME TWO DAYS when she heard a vehicle oming up the road. She was still jumpy, every little sound naking her nervous. She hated feeling afraid. She kept the loors locked all the time and found herself always looking outside as if she feared she'd see Griffin Crowley peering in hrough the frosted window at her.

She no longer felt safe in her home. She feared she'd be outting bars on the window and doors just like homes in big cities ind cursed Griffin Crowley to hell for making her feel this way.

At the sound of a vehicle coming up the drive, she looked out. The snowplow had been in earlier to clear the road again since the snow had continued for days now. The driver had old her that the deputy's patrol car had been removed from he ditch back up her road, that reminder at least now gone.

He'd said he just wanted to make sure she was all right and see if she needed anything. Rory thanked him and sent him on his way before going back into the house. She no longer trusted anyone who said they wanted to make sure she was all right out here alone.

The door to her bedroom was closed. She wasn't sure she could ever go in there again even though Georgia had come in with Faith Bailey and some friends and cleaned the room after the state investigators had finished.

Rory thought it might be Georgia who'd pulled up in the yard. Her friend had practically moved in over the past few days she was there so much.

But it wasn't Georgia. Rory saw Devlin climb out of the

back of a large black car. She caught sight of an older man in the rear and what appeared to be armed guards in the front.

As Devlin got out and closed the door, the car pulled away, leaving him standing out front.

Rory stepped to the front door, unlocked it and, opening the door, walked out onto the porch, hugging herself against the cold and the inevitability of Devlin's visit.

She'd been expecting him to come by and tell her he would be returning to his country. That's what princes who were destined to one day be kings did. She'd warned herself of this day, dreading it and aching to see him one more time.

At just the sight of him her heart took wing. She felt tears blur her eyes and quickly brushed them away. This was the man who'd stolen her heart, given her something so precious and saved her life. If he hadn't braved the storm to get to her...

He smiled as he climbed up the steps to the porch where she stood. She was a sucker for that smile. "You look so good."

She laughed. She knew she looked pretty bad, her bruised face discolored, her black eye still swollen.

His touch had the exact effect she'd sworn she wouldn't let it have. When he reached for her, she stepped into his arms as if she was coming home instead of saying goodbye. When he kissed her, Rory told herself she was only making things worse by kissing him back.

"You're freezing," he said and led her into the house.

Once inside, they stood facing each other in the living room, suddenly both seemingly shy and tongue-tied.

"You can't stay here," he said. "At least not for a while."

"I'm not staying." Her throat tightened around the words in a stranglehold. "I'm selling the ranch."

His look brought fresh tears to her eyes. "You can't sell this place. You can't let what happened erase everything that came before it. I know how much you love this ranch, what staying on it means to you."

Rory said nothing. Even if she could have spoken without crying, she wasn't sure what she would have said.

"I want to take care of you," he said quietly. "I want to marry you and give our child a name."

"What name would that be? Barrow? Or Wycliffe?" She shook her head. "You're a prince. I'm just a cowgirl. You belong in your country. I belong in mine."

He smiled ruefully. "I'm no prince. You can attest to the fact that I'm not even a gentleman." His hand dropped to her stomach, his palm warm.

She returned his smile. "You saved my life."

"You saved mine. If I hadn't met you…" She watched as Devlin stepped to the fireplace, reached behind one of the stones and pulled out some folded light green papers.

"What are those?" she asked, stepping over to join him in front of the blazing fire. She'd built the fire hoping it would scare off her chill. It hadn't.

"It's my original birth certificate. Evangeline had it stolen from my country's archives office."

Rory gasped as he tossed the papers into the fire. The flames licked over them an instant before the paper burst into flame and disintegrated before their eyes.

"Devlin, what have you done?"

"I've burned up any proof that I am the son of King Roland Wycliffe the Second."

"But you're the *prince*. You're to be the next king of your country."

Devlin chuckled as he pulled her to him. "I never wanted to be a prince, let alone a king. I'm a groom. All I know is horses."

"But your father—"

"He and I have spoken. We are in agreement about the future. It turns out that my father is a romantic at heart. He once loved a woman with a mind of her own—"

"Your mother."

Devlin nodded. "She was pregnant with his child, but unlike me, he made the mistake of letting that woman get away from him. He's regretted it to this day. I refuse to have that kind of regret."

She shook her head. "You would give up all of that—"

"To stay here and raise our child together? I already have, Rory. The only question is whether you will have me."

Devlin took Rory in his arms. "I love you. I love our baby. Rory Buchanan, marry me."

He looked into Rory's eyes. The most beautiful green eyes he had ever seen. Like priceless jewels. Rare as the woman.

He wished his mother was still alive so she could have known Rory. He knew she would understand the power of love. All she'd ever wanted for him was to be happy.

"You would give up being a prince? Give up your homeland?"

"My home is where you are," he said as he kissed her until she finally gave him what he wanted—a breathless yes.

Epilogue

Most things in that wintry part of Montana got back to normal after that.

Rory Buchanan and Devlin Barrow were married by the Justice of the Peace in Whitehorse. They honeymooned in Hawaii, where Devlin studied to become a U.S. citizen.

Back in Montana, there were only a few reminders of what had happened. A former sheriff's department guard was now driving a brand new four-wheel-drive pickup and throwing money around like he had it.

Just before winter really set in, a son was born to the princess in a home birth at Stanwood. Lady Laurencia was in attendance for the birth of Prince Roland Wycliffe the Third and received a king's ransom for it.

Within weeks, Evangeline and her son had returned to their homeland. Stanwood estate was put up for sale. The horses had already been purchased, and were being boarded at the Buchanan Ranch.

The palace sold much faster than anyone in town had expected. There was speculation on who'd bought the place and what he planned to do with it.

A huge garage sale was held that brought people from all over the world. The furnishings were sold at pennies on the dollar.

The biggest shock came that spring when one day the guard house was gone—and so was the palace as if it had been carried off stone by stone.

Wasn't long after that that the rumors were proven true. The whole place, horses, acreage and all, had been given to Devlin and Rory as a wedding present by King Roland Stanwood Wycliffe the Second.

"Do you think Lady Monique really killed Prince Broderick?" Rory asked her husband one winter night when they were curled up in bed together.

"Maybe. She was capable. But I think more than likely it was Princess Evangeline."

"She got away with murder?"

Devlin pulled Rory close. "No, I'm sure the king is familiar with the way Evangeline operates. She won't be beheaded or thrown in prison. After all, she is the princess."

"But surely she won't be allowed to get away with murdering your mother or her husband."

He shook his head. "She will be a prisoner at the palace, not allowed out of her chambers except to make the appearance of being a mother to her son, the next heir to the throne." Devlin kissed the top of her head. "Don't worry. Our child is safe."

He'd known from the moment his mother had been murdered and he'd sworn he'd get justice for her that he'd never be able to return to his homeland. His heart had ached at the thought.

But that was before he'd met Rory Buchanan. Her love for this land—and him—had healed that ache. He belonged there, with Rory and their unborn child. There was no place on this earth he wanted to be other than right here in Rory's arms.

"Any regrets? You could have been married to a prince," he whispered against her hair.

She laughed softly. "I am."

*Mills & Boon® Intrigue brings you
a sneak preview of…*

Kylie Brant's Terms of Surrender

*Targeted by a bank robber bent on revenge, hostage
negotiators and former lovers Dace Recker and
Jolie Conrad are reunited against their will. The
FBI has recruited them to draw out a killer, but their
close proximity to each other will draw out wounds
from their past. Can they heal their hearts for
a second chance at love?*

*Don't miss this thrilling new story in the
ALPHA SQUAD mini-series, available
next month from Mills & Boon® Intrigue.*

Terms of Surrender
by
Kylie Brant

Dace Recker donned the Tac-Vest with its heavy ceramic plates and fastened it. Grabbing his bag of gear out of the car's trunk, he slammed the lid and jogged toward the police tape establishing the outer perimeter around the bank. Ducking beneath it, he flashed his shield at the cop stationed nearest him and began to shoulder his way through the sea of law enforcement officers toward the Negotiations Operation Center, a converted ambulance, parked nearby.

"Dace!" Turning, he recognized Jack Langley from Alpha Squad, the SWAT unit his Hostage Negotiation Team was assigned to. Jack's limp was noticeable in his hurry. The injury he'd sustained in the explosion at the Metrodome last month still had him on the disabled list. At that moment, however, HNT leader, Bradley Lewis, stepped out of the NOC mobile unit and spotted Dace, waving him over. Jack caught up with him as he headed toward Lewis and said urgently, "Your new partner's here."

"Yeah?" Dace craned his neck, but could see no one standing near the commander. "Who is it? Have you met him yet?"

"Her. And she's—"

"Recker, where the hell is your team responding from, Siberia?"

Lewis's familiar impatient tone succeeded in snapping Dace's attention from Langley.

"What's the situation?"

"Bank branch with twelve regular employees, ten of them confirmed inside. Undetermined number of customers, but witnesses suggest at least eight. Someone managed to press the crisis button, which alerted police at 9:21 a.m. Subject went barricade shortly after."

Dace checked his watch. 10:12.

"Shots fired upon entry, and again fifteen minutes later," Lewis continued. "No visual yet. The blinds were pulled shortly after the first shots were fired."

"Injuries?"

"Nothing confirmed. The situation's locked down with a full perimeter established. Your new partner's inside the mobile unit, trying to establish contact. You'll be primary, but she's got plenty of experience, too. The phone lines have been disconnected. The gunman did accept the throw phone, but hasn't answered it yet."

Dace nodded as Lewis turned and strode toward the command center, a sleek black specially equipped RV. The man would serve as their command center liaison, exchanging information with the SWAT commander. As Dace reached for the door to the NOC unit, his progress was halted by Jack's hand on his arm.

"Like I was saying…"

"A woman partner. Yeah, I heard you. Eat your heart out, buddy." Dace shot a grin at his friend. "When you get back on duty, all you have to look forward to is Bazuk." The eerily silent tobacco-chewing Cajun was Jack's personal nemesis, primarily, Dace figured, because both men had more than their share of ego.

But Langley didn't take the bait. "Yeah, yeah, but there's something you should know. I saw her when I was in human resources filling out insurance stuff."

"Who, the new partner?"

"Yeah, and it's—"

"Langley!"

Dace hid a grin at the sound of SWAT commander Harv Mendel's familiar bellow from the command center parked a hundred yards away. As Langley turned in resignation, Dace opened the back door of the NOC unit and ducked inside. Mendel was going to want to know what the man was doing on-site when he hadn't yet gotten a medical release to return to duty. But Dace knew his friend well enough to figure the answer. With nothing to do but rehab exercises, Langley was going slowly crazy. A civilian might spend his medical leave at the beach. Jack spent his listening to the scanner.

The unit was nearly empty save for a slender blond woman, seated at the table. Most of the team must not have arrived yet. "Dace Recker," he said by way of introduction. "Have you made contact yet?"

Her back was to him, but he heard her say, "Hello. Whom am I speaking to?"

His heart stuttered in his chest. The voice was familiar. Too familiar. It still haunted his dreams. Prowled his subconscious. Summoned memories he'd done his damnedest to forget for the past year and a half.

Disbelieving, he raked her figure with his gaze, desper ately seeking a sign that he was wrong. This woman wa slimmer, wasn't she? Her hair a lighter shade than he remem bered.

But a moment later she swung around to face him an recognition struck him square in the chest. No matter how impossible it seemed, how cruel, it *was* Jolie Conrad. The onl woman he'd ever allowed close enough to get a grip on hi heart.

The same woman who'd ripped that organ out of his ches when she'd walked out of his life eighteen months ago, afte their world had shattered around them.

Her expression mirrored his shock. But she recovered first, holding out the cell. "Out of seven calls made, this is th first answered. Woman's voice. She's handing it over to th gunman."

He took the phone she extended as if it were a lifeline Speaking with the psycho inside the bank who was holding at least eighteen hostages was infinitely preferable to dealing with the emotional punch of seeing Jolie again.

Not just seeing her. Being partnered with her.

God help him.

"This is Dace Recker, with the Metro City Police Depart ment." It took more effort than it should have to keep his focu on the hostage taker at the other end of the line. "Am speaking to the person in charge?"

"You are. And I have to say, Recker, that you and you people are screwing up my day."

The voice was male. Authoritative. Native English speaker No trace of regional accents. Dace's assessments were in stinctive, made in quick succession.

He glanced at his partner. *Jolie.* His gut tightened. She' donned earphones and was listening intently to the conversa tion. "I'm here to give you a hand with that…" Deliberately he let his voice trail off. "Help me out, here. What's your name?"

"Names aren't important."

He kept his voice easy. "Well, they sort of are. I have to call you something, don't I?"

There was a moment's hesitation. "Just call me John."

"All right, John, talk to me. Are you all right?"

The question seemed to catch the other man off guard. "I'm fine."

"That's good. I'm very glad to hear that. I want to keep it that way, okay, John? How about the rest of the folks in there? Are there any injuries?"

"You don't seem to understand how things are going to work, so let me explain. I want a black SUV with tinted windows delivered to the back doors. Pull your perimeter back another six hundred yards. Too many cops around here. I'm feeling a little claustrophobic."

"I'll work on it. No one's coming in there, John, but we're not going anywhere either. Now this is a two-way effort. You want something, you have to give something in return. I really need the status on the people inside with you. How many are there? Are there any in need of medical assistance?"

"There's one past need of medical assistance," came the chilling reply. "And there will be more if you don't follow my directions exactly." The line abruptly disconnected.

Releasing a breath, he set the phone down. Only then did he transfer his attention to Lewis, who had entered the unit and slipped on headphones during the conversation. "Did you get that?"

Lewis took off his headphones and headed for the door. "I'll run the delivery-exchange angle by command center. If he reestablishes contact before I return, you know the drill."

Dace did know it. Stall him. Establish a rapport by using

active listening skills. Once command center okayed it, the team would work an exchange while getting concessions for the people inside. Releasing the injured. Sending in food. But this was the trickiest part of negotiation. He didn't know the gunman well enough yet to predict how he was going to react when Dace followed the usual procedures.

He slanted a glance to the woman at his side, who even now was looking at him, her blue eyes guarded. And he knew this case had been complicated beyond all measure the moment he'd heard her voice and come face-to-face with the past that still plagued him.

The open back door framed Dr. Ryder, their psychological profiler, who'd stopped to talk to Lewis for a moment. With an effort at keeping their privacy, Jolie spoke in a whisper. "I'm sorry about this."

His loins tightened, as if in conditioned response to that familiar smoky tone. He gave her a grim smile and lowered his voice, too. "For what? Sucker punching me with this partnership? For not returning my phone calls? Or for taking off without a word a year and a half ago and leaving me to wonder what the hell had happened to you?" He could hear the bitterness lacing his words, but was helpless to temper it. "Take your pick, Jolie. What are you apologizing for? For walking out of my life? Or for walking back into it?"

© Kimberly Bahnsen 2008

MILLS & BOON®
are proud to present a new series

Three dramatic and sensual tales of paranormal romance
available every month from June 2010

The excitement begins with a thrilling quartet:

TIME RAIDERS:

Only they can cross the boundaries of time; only they
have the power to save humanity.

The Seeker by Lindsay McKenna
21st May

The Slayer by Cindy Dees
21st May

The Avenger by PC Cast
4th June

The Protector by Merline Lovelace
18th June

INTRIGUE

Coming next month

2-IN-1 ANTHOLOGY

PEEK-A-BOO PROTECTOR
by Rita Herron

An abandoned baby in Samantha's care is the target of merciless kidnappers. Police chief John's sworn to protect the pair – even if he loses his heart in the bargain.

UNDERCOVER FATHER
by Ann Voss Peterson

Someone wants to harm the baby boy left aboard Reed's ship. Tenacious PI Josie can get answers. Could she also be the thing that's been missing in Reed's life?

2-IN-1 ANTHOLOGY

A VOICE IN THE DARK
by Jenna Ryan

A serial killer's brutal attack left criminal profiler Noah scarred and determined to hide from the world, until he met beautiful FBI agent Angel – the killer's next target!

TERMS OF SURRENDER
by Kylie Brant

Targeted by a revenge-obsessed criminal, hostage negotiators and ex-lovers Dace and Jolie are reunited. Yet can they heal their hearts for a second chance at love?

On sale 21st May 2010

2 FREE BOOKS
AND A SURPRISE GIFT

We would like to take this opportunity to thank you for reading this Mills & Boon® book by offering you the chance to take TWO more specially selected books from the Intrigue series absolutely FREE! We're also making this offer to introduce you to the benefits of the Mills & Boon® Book Club™—

- **FREE home delivery**
- **FREE gifts and competitions**
- **FREE monthly Newsletter**
- **Exclusive Mills & Boon Book Club offers**
- **Books available before they're in the shops**

Accepting these FREE books and gift places you under no obligation to buy, you may cancel at any time, even after receiving your free books. Simply complete your details below and return the entire page to the address below. You don't even need a stamp!

YES Please send me 2 free Intrigue books and a surprise gift. I understand that unless you hear from me, I will receive 5 superb new stories every month, including two 2-in-1 books priced at £4.99 each and a single book priced at £3.19, postage and packing free. I am under no obligation to purchase any books and may cancel my subscription at any time. The free books and gift will be mine to keep in any case.

Ms/Mrs/Miss/Mr _____ Initials _____

Surname _____

Address _____

_____

_____ Postcode _____

E-mail _____

Send this whole page to: Mills & Boon Book Club, Free Book Offer FREEPOST NAT 10298, Richmond, TW9 1BR